the WISH LIST

the WISH LIST

Dominika Caddick

Kettering 2024

First published as *Gajowy* in Poland in 2023 by DC Books.

Copyright © 2024 by Dominika Caddick

The moral right of the author has been asserted.

A CIP catalogue record for this book is available from the British Library.

ISBN: 978-83-967121-6-5

Author: Dominika Caddick

Copy editor: Małgorzata Giełzakowska

Proofreader: Jonathan Karl Burcham

Beta reader: Gary Dawson

Typesetting: Gabriel Wyględacz—Studio Akapit

Cover design: Dominika Caddick. The photo on the front and back cover belongs to the author's private collection.

To my hubby Graham—my favourite grumpy old git...

Monday, 19 September

The rumble of the engine in my Corsa faded. I pulled the key out of the ignition and leaned back in my seat with a sigh. I was about to get out, but a glimmer of a photo in the sun visor caught my eye and my heart dropped.

My mum was a beautiful woman. Time didn't manage to paint too many wrinkles on her face, and her shapely figure could be envied by many young girls. The sun setting over the Cromer pier gave her skin a glow, and the summer wind blew her hair. The smile she gave me just before I took this photo was joyful and still completely untainted by the disease that took her last breath less than a year later.

I loved this photograph and the memory it evoked, but seeing her face again only brought a heaviness in my chest that I had felt since her death. I slowly let the air out through my mouth and unconsciously rubbed my tired eyes, only to realise that I must have smudged my makeup in the process. I completely forgot about it. Today, I put it on for the first time since she had passed away. The face in the mirror looked back at me with no expression. Concealer and a thick layer of foundation did not hide the dark circles under my eyes. I was exhausted.

Completing all the formalities leading to her funeral from the list she had left for me gave me a tough time, and although I sorted out almost all the testamentary obligations in just two months, I didn't feel any joy from fulfilling her will. Organising the funeral and wake, and taking care of other official matters became the only way to survive the first days without her. A list of simple requests from banking to packing and putting all her clothes and belongings in the loft gave me a reason to get out of bed every day. There was only one task left, the strangest one, I have to admit. That's why I left its execution to the very end. To be honest, I didn't fully understand the purpose of it. I had too little information, and that made me feel nervous.

I took a deep breath and got out of the car. The old cottage had a forlorn air to it. The sad grey exterior felt like a relic from the past, its existence drained of life and joy. I let my gaze wander across the neglected pathway leading up to the building. It was like looking at a desolate dreamscape.

I knocked on the door, which opened after a long while with a loud creak. There stood a slim, tall man dressed in a grey hoodie and dark bottoms. His sharp facial features were partially covered by a pointed beard. Locks of curly, greyish hair fell on his wrinkled forehead. He squinted at me from under narrowed opened eyelids, and a grimace of discontent appeared on his face.

'Mr John Harris?' I asked, stepping back involuntarily half a step, intimidated by his height and unfriendly gaze.

'I'm not interested in your vision of my salvation or in the answer to whether God is love,' he hissed irritably.

'No! No! It's not that!' I stammered, taken aback by his hostile demeanour.

'I don't want the Avon catalogue either,' he added, ready to slam the door in my face.

'But sir! I'm Lucinda Blackbird, Maya's daughter,' I hurriedly blurted out, instinctively grabbing onto the door handle. 'My mum asked me to deliver this letter to you.'

I held out my hand with the envelope towards him, but he didn't reach for it.

The sound of my mother's name made an impression on him because he glanced at me sympathetically and shrugged his shoulders.

'Fine, come in,' he conceded, stepping back a little to let me in.

I took a step forward, captivated by the mysterious host and his lodging. I shut the door behind me and glanced around the dimly lit living area connected with a kitchenette. The sunlight was filtering through a narrow slit of partially drawn curtains in one of the two windows, illuminating the darkness. Mr Harris wandered over to the wooden table, gesturing at one of the chairs for me to take a seat.

I moved the chair as far away from the table as I could as if that would protect my nose from the intoxicating stench of the cigar left smouldering in the ashtray.

'Mr Harris,' I began, wincing involuntarily. 'I'm not going to take up much of your time. Just accept this letter, and I'll be on my way.'

I held out my hand with the envelope again, but the man ignored the gesture once more.

'You read it!' he grumbled and sat down on the edge of the bed nearby.

I narrowed my gaze in contempt. He had no right to talk to me like that! But I guess there was a purpose for this visit, and if he wanted me to read the letter, then so be it.

I wearily leaned back in my chair and tugged at the heavy velvet curtains letting in a warm ray of sunlight. I squinted my tired eyes to make out my mother's neat handwriting—her final words were etched in my memory forever.

Harris hissed and shied away from the light as if he despised it.

I took a deep breath and began to read out loud, trying to understand the hidden meaning beneath each word. What she wrote made little sense to me, but one thing was certain from the text—she asked Mr Harris to finish a novel he had started writing for her years ago.

'Fucking hell, your mother always had stupid ideas!' he growled when I finished reading the last words, angrily nudged his foot at the typewriter, which for some weird and wonderful reason was right next to his bed.

'I beg your pardon?!' I instantly felt offended. 'Excuse me, sir! My mum ...'

'I really can't be bothered to do any writing at the moment!' he interrupted me, completely oblivious to my agitation. 'I don't have time or willpower for any of that bollocks lately! Besides, my head has experienced no inspiration whatsoever for ages, plus I'm blind as a bat.'

Suddenly, I understood why I was the one to read the letter.

'I see,' I replied amicably. 'If you allow me, I will be happy to help. I work as an editor, so working on books is a pure pleasure for me. You can also record yourself on a recorder and I'll write it all down ... Many authors create the first drafts of their books this way ...' I explained promptly, and in an act of desperation, I folded my hands as if in prayer. 'I am very keen on fulfilling my mother's last wish. Please, sir ...!'

Mr Harris quivered as if something touched his neck, scratched the back of his head and then reached for a new cigar, though one was still burning in the ashtray. The next thing I saw was his grumpy face disappear in a cloud of thick smoke, which irritated my throat even worse.

'Do you have a laptop?' he asked. 'Since I gave Maya my word, and promises must be kept ... Let's get on with it.'

'Of course, I do!' I jumped up excitedly. 'Does that mean that you agree?'

'Do I have another choice?!' he laughed.

In an instant, I realised what I had got myself into. I will have to put up with his moody arse for a little bit longer than I had planned before this visit.

John got up and threw the tip of the cigar from the ashtray into the cold ashes in the fireplace.

'Come back tomorrow at eight o'clock in the morning,' he said. 'I expect you to speak as little as possible and do not—I repeat—do not bother me with any unnecessary questions. Roger that?' I nodded obediently, and he added, 'We need about a week and a few bottles of good whiskey.'

I didn't have a chance to respond to that last demand, as he rushed to the door and opened it wide, making it clear that he had had enough of my company.

I muttered goodbye and left. I hurried into my car, turned on the engine and drove away hastily, eager to get away from him and his stinky place as soon as I could. On the way home, I wondered how my mum could have been friends with such a grump. Both the building and its owner did not make a good impression on me.

***

Mum kept her past under wraps. I was stunned when one day she unexpectedly admitted that she had once published a novel and some short stories in various anthologies. I begged her to reveal the titles to me, but it was all in vain. No matter how hard I searched on the Internet, I couldn't find any trace of them. We talked about it several times until my mother confessed that she had published under a pen name, fearing ridicule and undue attention in the small village where she grew up.

My questioning made her uncomfortable, so eventually I dropped it. I believed that soon enough, we'd have plenty of time to get back to this fascinating topic, but sadly, destiny had different plans ...

***

Ever since my mother passed away, I have been diving into the trunks of memories she left behind. The more I uncovered, the more I realised that the image she had projected as a parent was just a façade, hiding her true self. It seemed that stepping into motherhood meant she had to abandon the life she had once known. We only ever had each other. My father abandoned us before I was even born, and never looked back. Whenever I asked about him, it would anger her to no end, and she'd snap at me with the same cryptic message: 'Some people don't deserve a place in our hearts any longer than footprints on sand washed by the sea waves.' When I was younger, those words didn't make sense to me, but as time passed and heartbreaks piled up, their meaning became all too clear.

***

My mother meant the world to me. She made every effort to ensure that I never lacked anything. She worked in the library and loved books so much that she surrounded herself with them, not only professionally but also at home.

Our house was bursting at the seams with piles of novels and endless sagas. She would read at any opportunity given. It was thanks to her passion that I fell in love with the written word. It was inevitable. I grew up in the love for literature, so it was no surprise when I graduated in literary studies and then secured an internship at a publishing house where I now work as an editor.

Every time I met my mother's gaze, I saw pride gleaming from her eyes—this only strengthened my resolve to keep pushing towards my dreams.

***

On my way home, I wondered whether Harris had become so grumpy with age or rather as a result of lack of contact with people.

When I first arrived in the village, I couldn't find my way to his house as easily as I thought I would. The thorp seemed to have only a few roads, but somehow, I managed to get lost within the first few turns. Eager to complete my mum's last request, I headed to the village convenience store near the church. The shop owner eyed me suspiciously as I inquired about Mr Harris's place of residence, and supplied more than just directions. It instantly became clear to me that the man did not win her sympathy. According to her, he arrived in the village last autumn. If the woman was to be believed, he had only a few suitcases of clothes and a typewriter with him. He stayed in a cottage by the lake, which used to belong to an ex-fireman called Bob, who passed away a few years back. Mr Harris rarely appeared in her shop and never bothered replying to the many invites posted through his letter box to join the weekly bingo and cake evenings held in the village hall. After a while, the only signs of his presence in Bob's place were smoke coming from the chimney and the sounds of some music on the lake.

Naturally, he soon became the latest addition to the local gossip.

***

After a dinner that I had been heavily craving, I poured myself a glass of wine and pondered over my new duties. With the prospect of having to visit the cottage regularly, it seemed sensible to rent a room somewhere near Mr Harris's house.

Furthermore, moving locations was not only to ease the travel time to the cottage but also a way of escaping the painful memories of my mother that still lingered in my home. It was late September, and I found an idyllic little B&B by the lake, located less than twenty minutes' drive from Mr Harris's house. In peak season, I doubted I would have had such luck, yet I thought of it as a much-needed change after such a testing time. Settling there for the next week or so, I could easily work remotely and find some respite from everyday life.

Tuesday, 20 September

The sun timidly began to break through the branches of the trees when I pulled up outside the cottage. As I stepped onto the porch, a sleek black cat hissed at me from the shadowy corner. I was about to knock on the door when a gruff voice called out from within:

'Enter! It's unlocked.'

'Good morning, Mr Harris,' I said as I entered the musty cottage, the bitter chill of neglect hung in the air. Shadows danced across the cluttered room, shards of fading light catching wisps of dust swirling through the gloom. The bookshelves laid barren like ribs picked clean of meat. 'I am here as we agreed.'

He eyed me sceptically, furrowing his eyebrows.

'What was your name, again?'

'Lucinda, but everyone calls me Lucy,' I replied confidently. 'My mother named me after her favourite author, Lucinda Riley.'

He snorted disdainfully in response. 'Lucinda?! What kind of name is that?!'

I merely smiled patiently and shook my head; this was a conversation I was well accustomed to having with strangers. After all these years, it still surprised people that Lucy could be short for Lucinda.

My companion was sitting at a wooden table hunched over a briefcase. He furiously scoured its contents as if looking for something specific, but he seemed to be too disorganised in his actions. I watched him as he picked up more papers and then held them at arm's length while squinting his eyes.

'Oh, for fuck's sake!' he exclaimed exasperatedly. 'I can't see a thing.'

'What are you searching for, Mr Harris? I'll help you out,' I offered, sliding my chair next to him and dropping my bag onto the backrest with a heavy thud. I sat down beside him, carefully pulling one of the pieces of paper from between his fingers.

'Call me John, please. Mr Harris was my father after all,' he muttered after a few moments of silence. Undeterred by the awkwardness of the situation, I dived into helping him find whatever it was that he was looking for.

With a swift movement, he shoved the briefcase towards me.

'Here you go, that's the whole manuscript of the book we have to work on. Probably the pages got muddled so you have to put them in order and read them to me.'

'Okey dokey,' I said enthusiastically, itching to start. Reading and editing are my favourite things in the world after all.

'Lucinda,' he said with contempt in his voice, leaning back in the old chair until it cracked. 'That's a bit of a crap name if you ask me.'

I smirked. It also crossed my mind once or twice before.

I leaned over the manuscript. Fortunately, the pages were numbered in each lower right corner with a pencil.

I at once got to work and started flipping through the pages in silent concentration. Harris didn't speak either.

'Done,' I said after a few minutes. 'What now?'

'Now you have to read it to me,' he replied, got up from the chair and sat at the nearby armchair. 'You brought the bottle as I told you?'

I gave him a nod of confirmation and reached into my bag for the bottle of whiskey.

'Pour me a glass, will ya? You know, to ease my pain while I have to listen to it.' And with a wave of his hand, he pointed to the cabinet by the sink where the dishes were drying.

'Sure,' I said sarcastically.

I found only one glass, so I poured some whiskey into a cup and drank it immediately. I struggled to suppress the mounting irritation as he issued command after command, devoid of the simple courtesy of uttering *please*. I hated it when someone spoke to me like I was a maid.

The amber liquid embraced my throat in its pleasant warmth, leaving a bourbon flavour from an oak barrel in my mouth.

'Ready?' I asked, sitting down on the edge of the bed.

John confirmed with a mutter, enjoying the alcohol.

I began to read. With each new page, I became convinced that the guy could write good stories. It's strange that I've never heard of him before. His language was rough, his words strong and his sentences full of content. The story drew me in so much that for a moment I forgot where

I was. I stopped only when my throat was completely dry. I drank a few sips of mineral water from the bottle I always carry in my bag and then immediately went back to reading.

The author of the story written on loose sheets of paper sat motionless, with his head resting on the headrest. He listened attentively, with his eyes closed, without commenting. From time to time, he would raise the glass of whiskey to his lips, then cough and grunt for a moment as if strong alcohol was irritating his throat.

'Do you mind if I smoke?' he asked at one point, in a manner as soft as I would never have expected him to have.

'No, go ahead,' I said. After all, it was his house.

'They're in a box on the dresser.' He nodded in that direction. 'The lighter should be there as well, and the ashtray in the sink.'

'Don't bother getting up then, I'll get it for you, shall I?!' I retorted.

'Thank you,' he replied when I handed him what he had asked for. 'And as you are already up, a refill would be nice. See, my glass is completely dry.'

'Anything else?!' I murmured. 'Maybe you need a blanket or a pillow?'

'Nah, you alright,' he snorted. 'Sarcasm doesn't suit you, kiddo.'

'Oh really?! And you don't ...'

'Hold your horses!' he interrupted me, bursting out laughing, which at once turned into a prolonged cough.

'You know I'm just taking a mick out of you to see how hard you will let me push your buttons.' He coughed up, still amused.

'You reached the limit two demands ago,' I replied dryly. 'Are all men so annoying at old age?'

'You little shit!' he grumbled and smiled. 'I see that the apple doesn't fall far from the tree. You've taken more than just your mother's voice but her character as well. And what did you mean by old age? How old do you think I am?'

'I don't know.' I shrugged. 'Seventy?!'

'What?! Tell me you're joking. You do realise that your mother was a year older than me! Don't you?'

'No way. That's impossible,' I replied, but when his face showed indignation, I added less confidently, 'Seriously?!'

'Seriously,' he snapped, lighting his cigar.

I sat down on the edge of the bed again.

'You must have had a really hard paper round then,' I blurted out. Truth be told, I've never been very tactful.

'It wasn't that bad!'

I was tempted to reach into my bag, grab a mirror and nonchalantly hand it to him so that he would finally realise his own rough appearance; but I quickly quashed the idea. After all, what good could a reflection do when his eyes were either sealed shut or simply too blind to see?

'Read on,' he ordered, letting thick smoke out of his mouth.

I again let myself get carried away by the story, but just after a few minutes, I heard a snoring resembling the rattle of an old engine in some old clunker. I shook my head in disbelief, waited a few moments, then tiptoed over to his armchair and took the smouldering cigar from between his fingers. I gently lifted the ashtray, which was already dangerously tilted on his knee, and then I stifled the cigar in it. I also put his empty glass on the table.

I decided to use the moment of unexpected freedom to look around Harris's 'estate'. There wasn't much to explore; almost the entire area of the place was occupied by one room. It had to fit a living room, a bedroom, and a kitchenette.

The only source of light in the room was coming through a small double-leaf window. It wasn't too bright, considering that the glass was terribly dirty. The old, torn curtain turned brown from nicotine smoke. In addition, a tiny window resembling a barrel was installed above the sink, but it was also covered. There were piles of books in every corner. They were probably left here by the previous owners, as their sheer number wouldn't fit into the few bags he had with him when he moved in. The books resembled unstable towers. They were a testimony to adventures created in the imagination of long-gone authors.

From the dust that settled on the countertop of the dresser in the corner of the living room, you could make a small snowman. The old mirror on the wall looked like a prop from a horror movie, in which some sinister figure appears, driving the main character of the film crazy.

Nevertheless, the room had everything a man needed to function. A bed with a metal frame, a large table, and next to it two wooden chairs with several broken balusters in the backrests. Under the table, there was a thick burgundy rug. Opposite the soot-shrouded, extinguished fireplace was a fold-out leather armchair, a high-gloss lacquered wardrobe and one chest of drawers that looked as if it had come straight from the 'Cash in the Attic' TV series.

A narrow corridor led to a small bathroom. The walls were covered in classic white subway tiles that went halfway up the wall, with basic white paint above. In one corner sat a toilet with an old fashioned toilet tank that was integrated into the wall to save space. Next to it was a pedestal sink, the kind with separate hot and cold taps, situated atop a narrow vanity. Above the sink was a medicine cabinet with a mirror on the front, the kind that swung outward to access the storage space inside. The cabinet held the usual assortment of toothbrush, toothpaste, soap, and medications. Along another wall was an old clawfoot bath with the enamel worn and chipped in spots from years of use. A plain white shower curtain could be drawn around it, though there was barely room to do so. The floor was a basic black-and-white checkerboard tile that matched the subway wall tiles. One glance was enough to tell that the bathroom was as neglected as the rest of the cottage.

I was surprised when I saw another door in the hallway. It was quite shabby with paint peeling off in many places, with a decent-looking brass handle. Wasting no time, I pressed it and pushed the door lightly. The door creaked so terribly that I jumped away.

'Broom, mop and bucket,' I heard unexpectedly behind me.

'Ehrm ... what was that?' I asked, completely confused.

'A broom, a mop and a bucket,' Harris repeated and lifted himself from his chair. As he got closer, I got a strong whiff of nicotine that had soaked into his thick hoodie. 'The corpses of my former lovers and enemies are normally buried behind the shed on the left, by the pear tree. Here I keep only a broom, a mop and a bucket. See for yourself,' he implied and then opened the door wide, presenting the contents of the dark closet. 'What did you think I had in there?!'

'I was looking for a broom, actually,' I explained trying to cover my snooping around.

'Why? Did you get an urge to tidy up all of a sudden?!' he mocked, smiling indulgently.

'You have a bit of a mess in here ... That's it. I have asthma and it's hard for me to breathe around here. I just wanted to give the floor a quick once over,' I replied smoothly because even though I didn't suffer from asthma, my throat was itchy from the dust floating in the air at all times.

'It's not that bad, stop moaning,' he grumbled.

'What the eye does not see, the heart does not grieve over.'

'Well, maybe you are right ...' he murmured, frowning his grizzled eyebrows, then went back to his armchair, so I followed him. 'Indeed, my eyesight is getting worse and worse.'

'Maybe you just need glasses?' I asked. 'Simply go to the optician's.'

'Oh my! You are so wise! Why didn't I think about that earlier? Genius!' he got irritated. 'The nearest opticians are in town, so how am I supposed to get there? Even if I had a car, I wouldn't drive blindly.'

'Bus maybe?' I suggested mischieviously.

'I don't want to be wandering around the village looking for a bus stop like a weirdo. And besides, it's none of your business!' He suddenly got angry.

'Well, it is a little bit of my business though because if you knew how to take care of yourself, I wouldn't have to help you and listen to your self-pity,' I growled also angrily.

His face reddened and he clenched his fists so tightly that I could hear his knuckles cracking. His nostrils parted as if a fire was about to shoot out of them. He fixed his hazy eyes on me, then walked over to the table and slammed the manuscript onto the tabletop.

'Seriously, get the fuck out, I've had it with you!' he roared, gasping like an enraged bull. 'Your wise opinion about me is as needed as a cock-flavoured lollypop!'

I growled under my breath. It was obvious that I had pushed his patience to the brink with my last comment. Grabbing my belongings, I made a beeline for the door. As it clattered shut, I could still make out his enraged roars from inside the cottage.

I cursed myself for having such a fiery temper. If only I could be less stubborn and learn to bite my tongue more often instead of spouting sharp jokes and insults at those who didn't deserve it. Despite this, I knew that wasn't going to stop me from finishing what I had started—writing the book and getting to the end of this story.

I concluded that maybe it'd be best if I made things right between us first—perhaps a bottle of whiskey would do the trick. Yes, that was it—time to put on my brave face and make amends.

I winked cheekily at my reflection in the rear-view mirror, revved the engine and zipped off towards the B&B. The endearing hostess guided me to my room on the ground floor, where I chucked my suitcase on the bed and fired up my laptop. After a few swift clicks online, I found an optician not too far from John's place. I called their number and left a message on their answering machine requesting an appointment as soon as possible.

Wednesday, 21 September

Immediately after dawn, the hosts' rooster proudly fasted from behind the window, spreading its wings on the windowsill of the room and snatching me from sleep.

Dissatisfied with the premature waking-up call, I buried my head under the pillow, hoping to fall asleep again. I gave up after a while and selected the Netflix app on my phone to watch the latest episode of *Chesapeake Shores*. Then I took a shower. Still wet, I ran out of the bathroom thinking that I heard the signal of an incoming call.

Perhaps it was John, calling me to make up? We exchanged phone numbers for easy contact. It turned out that someone had indeed called, although it wasn't him. I listened to a voicemail message left by the receptionist at the optician's. The woman informed me of the next available appointment which was on the following day at three o'clock. She asked if I still needed it, requesting confirmation of the visit by a text message on the number she phoned from. I happily confirmed.

Content with the outcome of my plan, I had a cup of coffee and got ready to leave. I jumped in my car and drove towards the cottage on the edge of the forest, uncertain what the day would bring but at the same time determined to make the most of it.

***

Sounds of trumpets and saxophones welcomed me upon my arrival, giving me a slight boost to carry on. It seemed that Harris liked jazz. Good on him, I thought, enjoying the music.

I walked towards the door and knocked on it—not too hard because I was a little afraid of John's reaction. However, the e-mail with the confirmation of the optician's appointment on my phone became my bargaining chip, which may be able to alleviate the unpleasant situation between us from the previous day. Feeling a surge of courage, I knocked again, this time harder, and pressed the door handle.

As I pushed open the door, a blast of music hit my ears. Harris was standing by the table, lost in his little world while sweeping up the mess on the floor. It was quite touching to see him so engrossed in this task. I leaned against the doorframe and smiled at the thought that this old git had a heart after all.

Blimey! Who would have thought that he would tidy up after I had said that it was hard for me to breathe because of the dust?

All of a sudden, he turned around, saw my silhouette in the door, straightened up and threw the broom in the corner.

'I'm annoyed by coughing,' he said as if making excuses.

'Then you should quit smoking cigars,' I blurted out without thinking, then laughed nervously because I realised I was starting to play the wise guy.

'You laugh like your mum used to,' he remarked and smiled. 'You're late. I thought we agreed to start at eight.'

'I wasn't sure you wanted to see me again after our exchange of opinions yesterday,' I admitted with humility in my voice.

'Well,' he sighed. 'Let's agree that we both got carried away yesterday. Let's stop biting each other heads off every step of the way, okay? After all, we have a mission to accomplish.' He winked at me and invited me to come inside with a quick hand gesture.

'As an apology, I have booked an appointment with an optician for you. Tomorrow at three o'clock in town,' I said proudly and shivered.

He looked at me as if he wanted to scold me, but for the sake of the alliance he had just made, he clenched his fists for a second, then exhaled slowly and said:

'Great, many thanks, kiddo,' he murmured. 'Make yourself at home. I'll finish what I was doing, and I'll make us both coffee.'

'Phew, it's a bit stuffy in here, isn't it?' I noticed, smelling digested alcohol after entering the room as he swept the rubbish from the floor onto the dustpan. 'Do you mind if I open the window?'

'Go for it,' he replied emotionless.

'I can see that last night didn't end up with just the one glass of whiskey?!' I asked critically, leaning my hip against the edge of the table at which he was kneeling.

'That's how it is when your favourite perfume is bacon grease ...' He chuckled and then added promptly, 'One glass would be a crime in broad daylight.'

'I thought we had a deal,' I said, looking condemningly at the empty bottle next to the bed.

'Sorry, mother! I can't remember everything, my head is not the same anymore. Old age and all that, you know.' He sneered, then grabbed his chair and rose upright with difficulty. 'Well, that would be enough physical activities for the day ...'

My nostrils filled with a strong smell of sweat mixed with digested alcohol.

'I'll make us coffee, and maybe you could take a shower?' I suggested, looking at my companion's pointed, heavily silver-plated beard, trying not to breathe through my nose.

He stroked the scar under his lower lip with his thumb and wrinkled his forehead.

'It's a deal, kid,' he agreed. 'It's time to take a piss and have a wash. Maybe I'll even have a shave this fine Monday morning.'

'It's Wednesday, actually,' I corrected him. 'Today is Wednesday.'

'Wednesday,' he mumbled discontentedly on the way to the bathroom. 'I lost two days somewhere again, for God's sake.'

'No big deal!' I laughed understandingly.

I strolled up to the 'ancient' gas stove in the corner of the room and carefully turned on the burner with its frayed switch. The aged kettle perched atop looked like a relic from the dark ages; I couldn't help thinking it held some hushed secrets that could describe its centuries-long journey from one household to another. Filling a bowl with soapy lukewarm water, I stood at the sink, washing up what felt like an endless pile of dishes that had accumulated in there for years. I then brewed two cups of strong black coffee and eagerly perused the books stacked near the fireplace. Although I knew I shouldn't keep them placed here, I thought this spot may just be their home after all.

My eyes widened as John appeared from the bathroom, almost unrecognisable. His clean-shaven face and slicked-back hair took a decade off him—those broad shoulders, a toned chest, and a tight black T-shirt didn't hurt either. *Good on you, Harris,* I thought to myself and smiled hearing my thoughts.

'Have you been diagnosed with ADHD?' he asked, looking around the room.

'I beg your pardon?!' I replied surprised, putting the book down. 'ADHD?!'

'You can't sit on your arse even for a minute, can you? You always have to do something.'

'Ah, that ADHD!' I laughed. 'Well, I guess you can say that I hate idleness,' I admitted.

'Thank you.'

'Don't mention it,' I replied, winking at him.

I think I must have surprised him with my bluntness because, for a moment, he did not know how to react.

Finally, he patted me clumsily on the shoulder, and in the process of walking past me, kicked the nearest stack of books, which scattered on the floor like fallen dominoes. We both threw ourselves to our knees at the same time to collect them and collided head-on.

'Oh shit!' I groaned with a laugh, grabbing my forehead. 'What is your head made of? Reinforced concrete?!'

'A little respect for the elders, you cheeky mare,' he replied, also amused. Surely, his head didn't hurt as much as mine did, but the impact made him sit on the floor. Shortly after, he started looking through the books. 'What a gem!' he said, wiping dust off the purple cover with his hand. 'Maya's book.'

'Maya's ...?' I asked in a daze. 'You mean, my mum's?!'

He nodded.

'I would love to read it!' I called, reaching out for the book.

With a defensive gesture, John brought it closer to his chest and covered it with his hands.

'Haven't you read it yet?' He looked at me suspiciously.

'For some reason, my mum hid her work from me,' I replied regretfully.

'Then I can't give it to you. Sorry. Maya must have had her reasons for it, we have to respect that,' he said with a tender note in his voice. My eyes unwillingly filled up with tears, so I started to blink repeatedly preventing myself from crying. Thank God, Harris can't see much these days. 'She was something else, your mum, kiddo,' he started without any hesitation. 'There wasn't a thing that she couldn't do. Strong, resourceful ... and her sense of humour was as black as her hair was when she was young.' He laughed. 'She didn't let anyone push her around. She had bigger balls than many of the blokes I know. But the stories she wrote were delicate like an angel's feather ...'

He shook his head as if he'd felt himself drift somewhere else for a second and started to gaze at the book he pressed against his chest so I couldn't see the cover.

'I've told her so many times to write something less feminine! I knew she could. But she was stubborn like a mule,' he continued. 'I've read all her stories anyway, because ...' He hesitated for a moment.

She had talent, I said in my mind.

'... she had talent ... as for a woman, of course,' he added with a smirk on his face. 'Did you know when we were young, we belonged to the writers' group "Ink-saners"'. He laughed unexpectedly. 'That name has stuck with me for good now, I guess. Probably half the village thinks I'm crazy.'

'Optimistic odds,' I said with a laugh. 'I think the whole village thinks you are a defective recluse beyond repair.'

'We went to various events,' he said as if he hadn't heard me. 'Then after a while, everyone went about their own business, and we went separate ways. But the time we spent together is always going to have a special place in my heart!' John's face lit up at this memory. 'Never mind, what was I saying ...?'

'That my mother had balls, but she wrote like a girl?'

'Well, yes,' he confirmed, then slipped her book behind the waistband of his tracksuit bottoms and got up from the floor. 'Okay, that's enough of the trip down memory lane, kiddo. Let Maya rest in peace without mentioning her all the time.'

I was instantly saddened. The longing for my mother grew bigger and bigger in me every day. The disease took her away from me way too quickly. She died just three months after her diagnosis. I was not ready for it. Anyway, how can you ever really get prepared for such a loss?

Harris quickly realised that he should have been a bit more careful with his words. He must have felt guilty because he gently grabbed my hand with his and said softly:

'Come on, kid, we'll drink our coffee outside. I want you to see something. Just put a jacket on, please.'

I grabbed my cup and strutted out of the door. John had already made his way to the forest path, a bright yellow line cutting through an array of autumn trees. An incline gradually rose, then fell sharply towards a shimmering lake below. I walked down the hill with eager feet, my heart pounding in anticipation.

At the edge of the lake, I was taken aback by its beauty. The water glistened beneath the sun's rays, reeds whispering a gentle tune in the background. The autumn colours seemed to have been painted on every surface; oranges and yellows dappling through the foliage like a masterpiece.

Harris stopped next to a wooden bench, one foot tapping eagerly against the ground. With a smile, I joined him, and we took in the scenery around us.

'It's beautiful out here.' I sighed after a long moment.

'Yeah, you got that right. Let's sit down, I want to tell you something,' he said and moved a little, making room for me. 'An indispensable part of life is dealing with the loss of our loved ones. With a bit of luck, the Grim Reaper pulls our plug first, and we no longer need to worry about anything. However, it is often the case that it is us who come to live with a great loss,' he said calmly with a warm tone. 'I know that as a fact just too well. A year ago, I buried my wife. The world I had known so far ended.'

'I'm so sorry,' I said, barely uttering the words through my throat. 'I know how you feel.'

'I know you know. Unfortunately, I don't have any good news for you, kid. After a year, I still don't know how to deal with it all, and it doesn't hurt any less than it did the day I lost her.'

I pursed my lips into a narrow line. I wanted to cry.

'I thought that if I sold the apartment, packed all our belongings into boxes, and donated them to the Red Cross so that I would not have to look at them ever again, it would be easier to live by myself ... I quit my job, and I laid my hat here.'

'And did it help? Leaving all your life behind?'

He shook his head.

'Well ... not a day goes by that I don't think about Laura. But being away from our places seems to let me just about get by. So I live in this forest rubble and wait for the day when I die. Because it's a rather poor existence ...'

'And the notion that time heals wounds is just utter bollocks?' I asked.

Harris stared at me, reading my expression and unspoken fears as if they were written in the sky. He gave me a fleeting glance of empathy before tenderly tapping his fingers against my wrist.

'Time only takes away our memories after a while ... It erases voices and images from our memory. That's about it.' He shrugged and finished the rest of his coffee with one gulp. 'Whiskey helps me sleep. Cigar smoke blurs the contours of the new, unbearable reality. Well ... that's how it works for me. Everyone needs to find their own way of numbing themselves, I guess.'

I pondered how to escape from my mundane existence. Nothing had worked so far. I was almost done with the seemingly infinite tasks mum had assigned to me, and a wave of dread washed over me at the thought of what life would be like once I finally finished everything on that list. What will I do next?

'We live in a world where there is no place for male pain and helplessness, such emotions are perceived as weakness ...' John continued with tones of sadness in his voice. 'It is a lot easier to lock yourself in the wilderness of the forest and pass as a freak than to try to explain to anyone that you want to shoot yourself in the head every day because you feel lonely.'

'But something is stopping you from doing it, isn't it?' I said before biting my tongue. Fortunately, the man did not consider it a gross tactlessness, because he let out a hearty chuckle.

'If I tell you what it is, you won't believe me, kid!'

'Oh, go on then!' I nudged him to the side with my elbow as a sign of encouragement.

'Have you met the old stray cat yet? I think he is hanging around here somewhere.'

'You mean that black cat? I saw him once on the porch.'

'It's Julian.'

I snorted and then looked back to see if the animal was watching us from the thicket of the forest.

'He would have died without me, that fleabag,' he said warmly. 'Anyway, we help each other. I feed him, and in return, he listens to my evening regrets and sobs.'

'I don't know what to say,' I confessed completely touched, and the first tear rolled down my cheek.

'Your mother was a force of nature, kiddo,' he declared and with a deep nod, gave me a permission to cry. 'She was happy, I know she was. She had everything she cared for near her. She wasted no time. I'm sure there are just a few things she regretted in her life.'

'How do you know that?'

'I just know.'

'And where does this certainty come from?' I asked. 'You said yourself that your pals group broke up and everyone went their own way ...'

'Because it did,' he admitted. 'But Maya and I remained friends.'

'Seriously? She never mentioned you,' I said suspiciously.

Harris sighed.

'It's because there was probably nothing worth mentioning ... The truth is that she visited us quite often for dinner or coffee. Your mum and Laura liked each other very much. She must have been friends with her, not me,' he laughed, stroking his thumb on his wedding ring. 'Two nutters ...'

'I didn't know anything about your wife Laura either!' I interrupted him and felt sad all of a sudden. 'I wonder how much more I don't know about my own mother ...'

'You probably don't know a lot about her,' he remarked and added, 'On the other hand, you know everything she wanted you to know,' after noticing my angry expression. 'So cherish what you know then.'

'Oh, thanks for that wisdom!' I said ironically, but he didn't take it that way.

'There's nothing to be thankful for, kiddo.'

I didn't quite know what to think. Why did my mother hide their existence from me? When did she visit them? What excuses did she use? After all, we spent most of our time together!

'It's beautiful out here ...' I repeated after a while, because nothing else came to my mind to break the silence between us. 'Did you bring me here because it's your favourite place?'

'One of the two. And somehow, I landed here by accident. I found my cottage on the Internet. The price was extremely low, for obvious reasons.' He laughed again. 'It's a sleepy village. It seemed to me that in a place like this, it would be easier to give up life. Unfortunately, Julian has prevented me from doing it for the time being.'

'So, you can say that you bought the property in a package with life support!'

'Something like that.'

'Where is that second favourite place of yours, which you mentioned?' I asked.

'Not too far from here, actually,' he replied, sighing. He tilted the cup upside down to shake the coffee drops out of it. 'But I haven't been there for a long time. Too many memories ... We called it no-man's-land.'

'Nice.'

'We started to call that place our own. Because I used to go there with Laura to revel in our own way: to de-stress after a hard week of work, rest, breathe the country air. It's a place in the middle of nowhere, without the Internet, phone coverage or any amenities. Perfect to be together in nothingness.'

'It's nice to have a place like that.'

'Indeed,' he agreed sadly. 'Come on, let's go back. Although it seems warm in the sun, the wind from the lake will pick up and I'll catch a cold, and I think you know how dangerous man flu can be. Once I hit the seventy mark, there are no more jokes with such ailments ...' he mocked my words from yesterday.

'Well, old age is no joy,' I grumbled.

'Come on, you cheeky cow.'

We climbed the path that now led uphill. Harris began to gasp with effort but walked next to me without slowing down. He was in good shape, although I didn't suspect him to be.

Julian was waiting for us in front of the house, sitting on the stairs. John scratched him behind his ear, then entered the cottage, and me and the cat followed. He handed me the manuscript and waited for me to sit down, then sank down with a dull groan in his chair. I expected that I would have to rearrange the pages, but—to my surprise—they were arranged in the right order.

'Do you still have much left to read?' he asked in a crooked voice.

'About a dozen pages,' I replied and immediately began to read.

This time he managed to stay awake. He did not comment, although he did sometimes grunt or snort hearing words that I read. Three quarters of an hour later, I turned the last page of the manuscript, John sprang to his feet and rushed towards the dresser. He pulled out a notebook and a pen from the top draw.

'Flipping hell, where did I put it?!' he was irritated as he rummaged through one draw after another.

'What?' I asked lucidly.

'I had a magnifying glass somewhere here ... Oh darn it, where would it be ...? I have to write down a few things before they escape from my head ... Oh, there it is!' He held the magnifying glass in his hands, feeling its weight that seemed greater than it actually was. Grinning from ear to ear, he raised it proudly as if it were a trophy he had just won.

He sat down at the table and began to write, following the magnifying glass in the wake of the pen. He wrote in large letters and quickly filled a few pages of his notebook. I could have sworn that his previously hazy eyes now took on a wild glow. Harris fell into a writer's trance.

Out of boredom, I put the washed dishes in the cabinets and wet-wiped all the countertops. Then I poured some whiskey into a glass and gave it to him. I sat on the edge of the bed and watched him for a while.

'Okay, that's that then!' he exclaimed unexpectedly after a few minutes and made me jump. 'Enough of these scribbles for today. I'm hungry.'

'Me too, we should eat something. How about some sandwiches?'

***

Our grand plans of getting down to work on the novel were instantly dashed when an old photo album appeared on the table. Puzzled, I wondered how these souvenirs had escaped the village's beady eye. The stacks of books belonged to him as well.

John told me some wild stories about my mother's youth while sipping his favourite liquor and smoking some cigars. It didn't even bother me that our faces were shrouded in a cloud of smoke. Surprisingly, it started to smell reminiscent of sun-drenched Cuban tobacco plantations.

I expected the stories would make me sad, but instead, I felt a strange peace as if the missing pieces of my mother's picture were being filled in by every word spoken. John's words lulled me into a sense of belonging, with memories that I could always keep close to my heart.

Thursday, 22 September

The optician's office door flung open, and I rose from my sturdy seat in the waiting area. John sprinted for the exit and didn't bother to wait for me. His face was contorted, a clear warning of his anger.

'And?' I asked. 'What's wrong with you then?'

'Coffee,' he barked like a dog.

'What?!'

'Coffee first, come on.'

'Do you want to go to a Café or McDonald's?'

'McDonald's is fine,' he grumbled, without slowing down.

'All right,' I agreed. I could hardly keep up with him. When we got to the car park, I dared to start asking, 'Did you get bad news? Why are you so angry?'

'I'm not, I just hate going to the doctors.'

'I understand that. What about the diagnosis?'

'I have a problem with refraction in my eyes. Supposedly, it's nothing too serious. Photochromic glasses will do the trick.'

'That's not bad news then, is it?'

'Well, no. I'm just annoyed. If I had known that's nothing, I would have sorted it out earlier.'

'True,' I remarked. 'When do we have to pick up the glasses?'

He must have been startled by the plural, he smiled at me and tapped me on the shoulder.

'The office will send them to me by courier in a few days.'

'Cool, that's good.'

'Let's go to get this coffee, shall we?'

The double espresso did little to rouse my companion into conversation. As we drove back, he stared out of the window as if captivated by every detail of the passing landscape. I wryly wondered if the mere prospect of getting glasses had somehow sharpened his vision. I understood his need for space. I couldn't blame him. After all, I too had recently become weaned from company. I dropped him off at his place and said goodbye without even leaving the car. Harris did not insist that I stay. I didn't blame him either. I also needed a moment for myself.

Since our conversation yesterday at the lake, I had lots of questions. I didn't understand why my mother never mentioned her long-term friendship with John. Not once did I hear his or Laura's name, in any of the stories she was telling me over coffee or evening drinks.

I decided not to go back to the B&B but to go home. I certainly wouldn't be able to drift off anytime soon; my heart was pounding, and my mind was racing. The old dusty attic had a few boxes that belonged to my mum, so I thought maybe I'd find something that could connect her to the Harrises. Was it possible they had an affair? But why would she keep it from me? Did she think I couldn't comprehend something like that? It all seemed so mysterious ... When I arrived home, I wasted no time, went straight to the attic and spent some time up there, meticulously searching through all the boxes and chests I hadn't opened before.

After a while, I finally found something. It was a small notebook in a leather binding, tied with a leather cord. A diary! I sat on the dusty floor, anxiously flipping through the pages.

First dozen of them, it seemed like my mother admired a man called Luke. In her youthful love, she dwelt on his beautiful face, as well as on how he captivated her with his refinement, great sense of humour, and impeccable manners. She couldn't believe that a boy could be so generous in showing affection. Soon she described a few very passionate scenes between them. Their detail made me blush. I felt quite awkward reading about such intimate matters, so I only looked at the following pages briefly. I was looking for John's name to appear among the pages, but my mother had only mentioned Luke.

The notes stopped unexpectedly after a few months of their relationship without explaining why. I gathered that the lovers began to spend so much time together that she simply didn't have enough time to write a diary. Mum only made it to half of her notebook. Disappointed, I made my way down to the kitchen to make myself a cup of tea. My throat was parched, and I felt a tickle of dust on my tongue. Finding my mother's diary raised my hopes, but it was filled only with confessions of a young woman in the throes of love.

I didn't want to miss anything, so for peace of mind, I turned the notebook upside down, trying to shake out something that might have been pushed between the pages. Unfortunately, nothing fell out. So, I started checking, page by page, of the unwritten part of the diary. I was hoping to find some sort of address, a phone number … I hoped that such things didn't just happen in movies.

I was near the end when I found a few written pages. I was struck by the name I could see everywhere. I felt hot with the impression.

I'm trembling as I write these words, fearful of the consequences should anyone else discover my inner turbulence. Johnny and I made a pact to never discuss what happened that day. It's a vow that we both must keep, or our shared pain will be unknowingly inflicted to others. I wish this was all a bad dream, but reality has seeped into my core like an icy chill I can't shake off. My world feels broken and I'm desperate to find solace in knowing it won't always be this way.

I write this in tears as I recall the last six months of my life. How could he, my own lover, change so quickly? How could his hands which knew how to make me feel loved and adored also be capable of hurting and bruising me?

He would come home drunk and take out his rage on me, leaving me with aching ribs and swollen lips. Every morning was followed by repentance, promises of change, and pleas for forgiveness. I felt like I was bound to him emotionally and unable to escape. I kept these bruises hidden from everyone around me, ashamed and scared to tell anyone the truth.

It had to end. But it never should have happened the way it did.

The waning weeks of summer brought us to this beachside resort. Lively music from the group Boney M attracted Luke and me to the disco. It had been many days since he last drank, a feat I was proud of but still anxious about. Dinner was delicious and conversation buoyant. We laughed and danced, surrounded by people as if on a cloud of energy and joy.

Then came unexpected guests. His friends from work brashly filled the air with alcohol-laden laughter and snide comments.

The cracks in our fun widened with each movement they made, their vulgarity consuming what little innocence remained of that night's atmosphere. As I watched Luke trying hard to keep it together, a wave of sadness washed over me.

I begged Luke to go back to the hotel, but he just laughed it off. I refused to be a part of the drunken mayhem. My words were laced with maliciousness as I warned him that if he planned to return drunk, I wouldn't open the door for him. With my heart pounding in my chest and anger bubbling inside me, I marched back to the room. But I underestimated Luke's mania of showing off in front of his mates. He followed me, trying to prove that he was worthy and strong enough to discipline me. I managed to break free from his grip, but suddenly he came running towards me and punched me right on my lower lip. Blood seeped through my blouse as I hid my face within it and ran towards our apartment. All I could feel at that moment was humiliation and sadness. I walked to the room and collapsed on the bed sobbing. Tears rolled down my cheeks as the memories of all those promises made by Luke flooded my mind. After some time passed, exhaustion finally won, and I drifted off into a deep sleep.

The sun had not even begun to rise when I awoke. Luke was still out, and I feared the worst. With a heavy heart, I ventured off in search of him. All that remained in the wake of Saturday night's revelry were empty beer bottles lying strewn on the grass and a smouldering fire pit near the lake shelter. To my dismay, I found him sleeping on the marina by the lake, and no matter how hard I tried, I could not wake him up. Nor *could I lift him from this spot. Desperate for help, I ran to the nearest telephone box and phoned Johnny with my plea for help. His tone was weary but understanding; he told me to stay put at the marina and watch over Luke to make sure he did not start choking on his vomit during his slumber. It felt like an eternity before John arrived at the scene, bleary-eyed and perturbed at being woken up so early on a Sunday morning.*

I felt my heart stop as he stepped closer. When he saw my broken lip, the anger in his eyes was something I had never seen before. His gaze moved to Luke, sleeping behind me on the ground, before dragging me by the hand down the path leading away from Luke. We walked together in complete silence, with only Johnny's heavy breaths filling the distance between us. When we arrived at my apartment, he told me to make a pot of coffee and prepare a bed for Luke—he promised he'd bring him back shortly. I tried not to show how much pain I was in when he tenderly touched my cheek but despite all my efforts, I started to cry hysterically. I went to hug him searching for some comfort, and my shirt lifted up slightly, revealing the bruises on my ribs from my last attack from Luke. He opened the door to the stairs and ushered me inside without saying anything. He hurried towards the lake while I watched him, feeling an overwhelming sadness deep within me.

Standing in my apartment, I felt my heart sink. John's furious face came into my mind, and I knew this would lead to trouble. A deep sense of dread took over and I quickly ran back outside.

I raced towards the pier, where I was met with a scene of chaos. Luke was drunkenly staggering around, completely unaware of the danger he was in. Johnny had a long history of boxing, making his fists more powerful than steel, and drunk Luke seemed to be no match for him. I watched as they started to throw punches.

I got in between them and desperately tried to part them. Luke brushed me away, and I stumbled, my hands and knees taking the brunt of my clumsiness. John was a vision of rage, lashing out with force as he hurled his foe into the deep waters below. He then helped me up and barred me from trying to part them again.

'That's enough, Maya!' he hissed. Words I will always remember. Before I could say another word, he dived into the dark depths below. All that was left in their wake was an eerie silence. Fear began boring into me as I stood frozen on the marina.

My heart raced as I let out a desperate howl. I wanted someone to hear me but felt so insignificant in this vast expanse of water. I saw a small boat bobbing in the distance and pleaded for the fisherman to come to my rescue.

John was the first one to come up to the surface, with my help, he hoisted Luke up onto the marina. He lay still like a corpse already taken by death. I wept and shouted for assistance, the fisherman radioed the emergency services. Medics rushed to Luke's aid, while police officers questioned me and John relentlessly about Luke's whereabouts. John had to speak for me, as I was too distraught to utter a word. At that moment,

I felt so helpless when all my efforts amounted only to pulling his lifeless body from the depths of the lake.

I sat quietly, like a stone statue, and was receptive to what the fisherman said. His words sank deep into my soul as he confirmed John's version of events.

Soon after, I heard a deafening silence as they announced Luke's death. All I remember next is waking up in the hotel room, feeling completely sick with regret and sadness.

As I slowly lowered my legs from the bed, I could feel every joint aching and throbbing. John and Laura were sitting at the table when our eyes met. Although no words were exchanged between us, I felt the sorrow we shared—the sense of guilt we all carried for not being able to do more to save him.

The writing stopped, and I sank into the chair I sat on. For a moment, I was still covering my mouth with my hand in amazement.

Is this true? It was hard for me to believe it, but my mother wouldn't lie about things like that, would she? My analytical mind demanded information, I had to get to know if Harris remembered these events the same way. I had to find out the truth. Mum was dead, and so was Laura. There is only one witness of those events left. I needed more details and only John could give them to me.

It was already dark outside. I had almost a three-hour drive to his house. I should let go of it all for this evening. I knew I should, but ... how could I? I know I would struggle to sleep tonight with all this rattling around in my head. And if I wasn't getting any sleep tonight, why should he?

I picked up a can of Red Bull from the fridge and took a few sips at once. I was about to leave the house when I decided to go back to the kitchen to get a bottle of gin, just in case I needed it later to ease my mind. I put it in my bag with my mother's diary and hurried out of the house.

***

I pulled up outside John's cottage at ten minutes to eleven, my heart raced in anticipation. I'd rehearsed my questions a million times in the car, and now it was time to get answers. I marched through the door without so much as a knock and found Harris poised in his chair like a startled cat, he scrambled out of his seat, with shock written across every corner of his face.

'What the hell?!' he shouted, trying to identify the figure in the doorway.

'Funny that, I was about to ask you the same thing!' I hissed, approaching my companion, stunned by my intrusion.

I threw my mother's diary on the tabletop.

'What is it?' he asked, sinking into his chair.

'You tell me!'

I opened a few cabinets before I found the right glass and sat down next to Harris, who appeared confused. 'Are you having a drink or what?'

'Yes,' he murmured, reaching for the bottle beside the chair. 'Want some whiskey?'

'No, I prefer gin, thanks,' I replied, pouring it generously into my glass.

'Can you tell me what I owe the pleasure of such a late visit tonight?' he asked with a sigh.

'Of course,' I said wryly. 'I brought you my mother's diary. She wrote a very interesting story about a man named Luke ... Does that name ring a bell?'

John's face did not show any signs of surprise. He sighed and nodded his head, confirming.

'You know it does. I probably could guess what Maya scribbled in there,' he said completely unfazed. 'Just can't think of a reason why she would document any of those events. This can only bring problems when it falls into the wrong hands.'

'After such a long time? I don't think so, but I have to admit that this story shocked me a bit, to be honest.'

'I'd be surprised if it didn't, love.'

'Let's cut the small talk! I have a few questions to ask,' I said, taking a gulp from my glass.

'Ask away then.'

'Luke ...?' I started.

'... Cole,' he finished. 'He was an asshole. Your mum didn't deserve the way he treated her. No woman deserves that sort of treatment. Your mother loved him, and that was her weakness.'

'Yeah, she did write about it.'

'I lost control of myself and ... it turned out as it did,' he confessed without a trace of remorse. 'If you want to know if this event weighed on my conscience since it had happened, my answer is NO. I do not regret for a split second that that fucker did not come out of it alive.'

'Strong words,' I said wryly. 'You could have saved her in some other way: take her to a safe place for a while, report him to the authorities ...'

'As I said, I'd lost control,' he repeated.

'Well, we already know that,' I bleated out as the alcohol started buzzing in my head.

'Believe me, Lucy, it was for the best. Now I know that for a fact.'

'What do you mean by that?' I demanded.

'Is there a date in her notes?' he asked, frowning.

'No, she just mentioned that it all happened at the end of the summer.'

'It was the end of August 1994. And you were born in March 1995, right?'

'Yes,' I confirmed puzzled. 'Eighteenth.'

'You do the math.'

'Holy shit!' I shouted, shaking my head in disbelief.

'Maya was eight weeks pregnant when it all happened.'

'You killed my father!'

'I drowned your mother's torturer,' he drawled out through his clenched teeth. 'Who treated her like a piece of shit, even when she was already pregnant, kiddo. You can say that I gave you a chance for a normal life. I know how it sounds ... You may even hate me for saying it, but today I would do exactly the same thing.'

'I don't hate you,' I confessed. 'I'm just shocked. I didn't expect such a turn of events ... Also, I can't believe that the truth didn't come out about it, somehow.'

Harris spread his hands in a gesture saying that he could not believe it himself.

'You know, it was the nineties, small village ... Drunk drownings were not worth much attention of law enforcement. Besides, there were no witnesses ...'

'But what about mum?! How did she deal with it all, you know, after?'

'She found out about the pregnancy shortly after the funeral. At first, she thought she felt nauseous because of what had happened. She went to the doctor's and shortly after that visit, she disappeared from everyone's sight. I received a letter from her a few weeks later. She wrote about her bump and that she had moved back to her hometown to be close to her family.'

'What a story ... Jesus!' I whispered and poured the rest of the gin from the bottle into the glass.

'So now you know,' he said.

'Yeah.'

'What now?'

'Nothing. I just know, and that's it.' I drank the rest of the alcohol in one swig, nearly making myself throw up.

'Why did you do that for, you silly cow?' He laughed, looking at me indulgently. 'It looks like you will be sleeping here tonight, you little pisshead ... Bedtime for you soon, I'll sleep in the chair.'

He grabbed my arm and pulled me to the bed, curtly telling me to get some rest. I shot him a glare, kicked off my boots, and plopped them down beside the bed-frame. The room was beginning to spin, so I lay back and squeezed my eyes shut as the heat from the fireplace filled the room—making me feel even dizzier. Tears welled up in my eyes as I realised just how drunk I'd got.

'Did you eat anything today?' he asked, looking at me with pity.

'I don't remember,' I mumbled. 'I guess I just had breakfast ...'

'Gin on an empty stomach! That was wise as hell, love.' He shook his head disapprovingly. 'Do you want a sand-wich? Or maybe a sausage roll?'

'Sandwich and a glass of water, please.'

'How about a blanket and a pillow?' he mocked, refer-ring to what I said during our second meeting.

'No thanks, a sandwich will do ...'

I never did get that sandwich, drifting off into slumber.

Friday, 23 September

The sound of tires passing on the gravel woke me up un-expectedly. I sprang to my feet and looked around in panic. I calmed down a bit seeing the familiar surroundings.

A cup of coffee still steamed on the table, spreading the familiar aroma of morning around the room. I was laying on the bed, covered with a dark blanket. I was all alone.

I rushed to the door with a terrible feeling that someone had stolen my car. But it was still exactly where I had parked the night before. I must have heard another vehicle. Fresh tire tracks were visible on the path. They were much deeper than the ones my car had left behind.

So, I hadn't dreamt it, I thought and went back to the house to have the cup of coffee and then went around the grounds, thinking Harris must have gone to his favourite spot by the lake, but I didn't find him there. His absence seemed strange to me, to say the least. Although I did not know his morning routine too well, he once said that due to the problems with his eyesight he didn't go too far from his house.

Maybe he went to get something for breakfast? But where did these tire tracks come from? Strange ... I thought.

The excruciating headache pounding at my temples with the force of a sledgehammer reminded me why I usually try to abstain from alcohol. But then again, learning about my mother's tumultuous past was not an everyday occurrence. My throat felt parched, and I longed for a drink of cold water as I staggered back to the house. Then with my bag in hand, I set off on foot towards the village shop.

The nosy shopkeeper looked at me unfavourably.

'We don't appreciate making our village a drifting car show!' she said, wiping the counter with a grey cloth.

'Excuse me?' I asked, confused. 'Have you seen John today?'

'Yeah! That's what I'm saying. He went somewhere with those thugs ...'

'What thugs?' I asked surprised.

'Well, the thugs who made so much noise in drifting with their black Mercedes!' she said disgruntled and gave me a look as if she suspected I had something to do with it. 'They almost drove into me as I swept the path in front of the shop ... The postman told me that they barely made it on the bend near the church.'

'And Harris was with them?'

'Yes. On the back seat.'

'Thank you very much,' I said and started heading towards the exit.

'We don't need this sort of scenes here!' the woman shouted behind me. 'In our village people prefer a peaceful life ...'

'Of course!' I agreed, barely holding back a smile. 'Have a nice day!'

I returned to the cottage. I wondered why John had to leave so suddenly. And with whom? In fact, I didn't know much about him. We met just a few days ago. We spent most of our time talking about my mum and memories from their youth. I didn't know what he was doing in his adult life, and if I should worry about him or just wait for him to come back.

I decided to dig a little in his belongings. I meticulously searched all the drawers of the dresser, wardrobe and suitcases under the bed, but I failed to find anything special or of any importance.

I slumped into the chair and reached into my bag for my phone to check for any messages. Just as I pulled my hand out, the bag slipped from my grasp, its contents spilling out across the hardwood floor. I cursed under my breath, trying not to disturb the stillness of the room as I leaned forward onto one knee to retrieve the items. But as I moved, a sharp pain shot through my leg, causing me to pause and look down at the floorboards beneath me. To my surprise, something was peeking out from underneath the carpet in front of me: a rusty metal deadbolt locked with an old padlock.

Excitement bubbled inside of me, I kicked away the table and quickly yanked back the rug. With no key in sight, it seemed that smashing the lock would be my only way to see what was hidden underneath it—but with what? In a fit of frustration, I clambered outside in search of a solution. And there it was—an old shovel propped up against the wall of the shed next to the pear tree. Vexed yet determined, I grabbed it and marched back towards the house.

I paused mid-stride, the shovel now a mighty weapon in the face of this unknown terror. My heart raced and my mind swirled with doubts; could I break this padlock? Would John judge me if he knew what I was trying to do? What horrors lay beyond the door? What secrets?

Breaking into someone's cellar alone. Did I have a death wish? I shook my head free from those thoughts, preparing myself for what could come next.

My curiosity was unstoppable. After a few swings, the latch cracked open, and the padlock fell to the floor with a thud. I grabbed my phone and activated the torch. Wooden stairs lay beneath, they rolled away with an air of intimidation, but I was determined to continue. My heart thumped in anticipation as I descended into the unknown—just like my namesake Lucy must have felt walking through the wardrobe in *The Chronicles of Narnia*.

The walls around me were adorned with peeling paint, which gave the scene an eerie feeling that sent a chill down my spine. I could smell the damp and cold from the front; a stark contrast to the warm autumn colours outdoors. With a burst of confidence, I desperately reached for a light switch on the wall. To my surprise, a single bulb illuminated near the ceiling, offering me just enough light for further exploration.

My pulse raced, and my palms were slick with sweat. I descended into the cellar, trying to quell the sense of dread that was building within me. It resembled a madman's lair, yet I couldn't bring myself to flee from the grisly scene. Papers and folders with names scribbled in black ink were strewn across the desk like little graves; each one more terrifying than the last. Photographs of men hung on a corkboard to my left, their faces too familiar for comfort. Written in red marker beside each portrait was a date and name—seemed like poor souls who had fallen victim to the killer's sadistic game. Despite of myself, I couldn't help but touch them, tracing my fingers over their faces.

I couldn't decide how to process this chilling discovery. Who were these men? Why were their faces staring at me from the walls of John's cellar? My curiosity was piqued, and I reached for my phone to take pictures when I heard a heavy stomp from above.

Fear rose like bile in my throat as a familiar figure descended the stairs. It was him as unmistakable as ever. His menacing black boots, his stormy eyes, his wrathful expression—it was John.

'Get out of there, now! Or I will drag you out myself, you nosy git!' I heard him shout.

The sight of his face totally swamped with anger completely paralysed me. I couldn't budge, I even stopped breathing. The man must have noticed that I was terrified, for he said more quietly:

'Lucy, please come upstairs. Don't keep me waiting.'

'I'm coming,' I replied, plucking up the courage. I didn't know what to expect from him. Ostentatiously, I grabbed the letter opening knife from the desk that wouldn't help much, but I felt a bit more confident, holding it behind me.

'Come on! Don't act like a fool, I won't do anything to hurt you!' he said and moved away from the stairs.

Suddenly, he groaned and leaned against the wall. I looked at him uncertainly. Only then did I notice that a trickle of blood was oozing from his cracked lip. He also had a cut above his eyebrow and a swollen eyelid and could hardly open his right eye. The left one seemed to be hazy, completely expressionless.

'Sit down!' I ordered, and he obediently sat down by the wall. 'Do you want some water?'

He shook his head weakly.

'Just give me a second, I have to catch my breath.' He sighed.

'I'm sorry, John. I don't know what I was thinking going down there,' I said remorsefully.

I felt very stupid. What came over me to search the house of someone who trustfully took me under his roof? After all, everyone has their secrets and sometimes it's better if they never see the light of day.

Harris shook his shoulders, breathing deeply, letting the air out slowly through his mouth.

'But ... you must admit that not everyone has a cellar hatch under the carpet in the living room ...' I broke out. 'What do you need this place for?'

John tried to get up, supporting himself with his hands. I grabbed his arm and helped him up.

'What can I tell you ...? You probably think you already know everything,' he grunted as we walked towards his bed. He slumped onto it with a sigh, his hands clasped over his head. I quietly opened the medicine cabinet and retrieved the first aid kit and a bottle of whiskey. My cheeks flushed as I slid the letter opener into the cutlery drawer. John side-eyed me with one eyebrow raised, disbelief written in his gaze.

'So? Shouldn't you be driving away with a screech of tires?' he asked.

'I'll try my luck and stay,' I said, sitting down next to him. 'Show me your face ... what did you get yourself into, eh?'

I soaked the gauze in hydrogen peroxide and washed his eyebrow and lip with it. I could see that I was causing him pain, although I was very gentle, but he did not even flinch. At the bottom of the first aid kit, I found a few strips for closing wounds and dressed them as best I could. I took some painkillers from my bag and put them on the table. John squeezed a few out of the packet, grabbed a bottle of whiskey, and headed for the door.

'You're welcome! No need to say thank you!' I shouted sarcastically.

'Thanks,' he muttered casually in the doorway and left, slamming the door behind him.

That was just too much for me. I flew like a slingshot after him.

'You ungrateful asshole!' I shouted. However, he did not pay the slightest attention to my words and walked towards the path leading to the lake.

I stalked after him with my heart pounding and rage building within me. I knew this was the perfect opportunity to confront him. He looked weaker than ever, dishevelled and confused, and I felt my strength growing. With a surge of energy, I watched as he stumbled over to his regular bench, clumsily shoving a few pills into his mouth before washing them down with whiskey. I was amazed at his recklessness.

'I came here for one reason only. To fulfil my mum's will,' I said, standing in front of him. 'You were supposed to be another point to check off the list. And somehow you managed to suck me into your world like a bloody Dyson. I deserve an explanation. Now is the best moment.'

'This is NOT the best moment,' he hissed without looking at me. 'I'm too pissed off!'

'YOU are pissed off?!' I shouted, raging with anger. 'Are you taking the mickey out of me?!'

'I don't really want to talk to you, kiddo,' he said calmly, not taking his eyes off the surface of the lake.

'You don't feel like fucking talking ... Wow, that's rich!'

His calmness drove me crazy. I clenched my fists, barely stopping myself from punching him. I stood by the reed-covered bank, swearing in helplessness.

'They found me because of you!' I heard behind me. I turned around. He no longer looked calm. His face filled up with anger. 'Before you showed up, everything was going my way, but you and your brilliant ideas ruined everything ... You screwed up everything!' he roared, hitting the back of the bench with a clenched fist.

'I screwed up?! How?!' I was screaming too; I couldn't let him push me into a corner. 'You know what?!'

'What?'

'Go back inside your shithole and die!' I hissed and walked towards the path, not letting him have the last word.

I lunged into the house, hastily shoving my belongings in a bag. Not wasting any time, I raced to my car and drove away, leaving a trail of dust billowing behind me. At the B&B, I rushed in and out of the shower before packing up and checking out. Furious and disappointed that I was unable to complete my final task, I made my way home—back to reality, to my day-to-day duties. To be honest, I had some serious catching up to do at work. My boss had been expecting the first draft of the novel I was editing for them days ago, and I was far from finished. With exasperation, I remembered the painstaking process that lay ahead; it was going to take day and night if I wanted to make the deadline.

***

The next seven days were a blur of work. I threw myself into the storyline and crafted vivid scenes to keep me occupied. It wasn't enough to distract me from my feelings of failure, but at least it meant I had less time to think about what had happened in that cellar. Images of John Harris's face replayed in my mind like a broken record, each looped phase more powerful than the last. The conversations between us had been full of secrets and hints, and all the details around him made me question everything.

This one man could hold so much power over me, but he no longer held any sway. I was no longer going to let this emotionally draining connection continue.

Saturday, 1 October

I went out to the porch with a cup of coffee, wearing a plush dressing gown and warm slippers. Mother Nature welcomed me with a sunny morning, probably one of the last this year, I decided to catch some sun in peace. I sat on the swing, curled up my legs, wrapped myself in a blanket, and immersed myself in my favourite book. Alice Walker again led me through the poignant story of Celie, who in her letters to God, in a cheerfully clumsy style, told the tragic story of her life.

'*The Colour Purple.*' I heard a familiar voice. I was so absorbed by the story that I did not realise that Harris managed to sneak up so close to me. His presence caught me completely off guard, but somehow, I successfully concealed any sign of fear, though a blend of surprise and irritation prevailed.

'What are you doing here?!' I asked, lowering my feet to the floor and straightening my body up unconsciously.

'I came to talk.'

'Talk?! And how did you know where ...?'

'Where you lived?!' He laughed mockingly. 'Do you honestly think it was hard to find a woman named Lucinda in this little town of yours? You should thank your mother for such a unique name.'

'If you came here to scoff, I suggest you turn around and get lost. I don't feel like arguing,' I hissed brusquely, pretending to be unmoved by his presence, though anxiety raged in my soul.

He wasn't going to give up so easily. Instead, he climbed onto the terrace and stood in front of me. He leaned his back against the ivy-covered lattice and crossed his arms on his chest.

'I am not here to argue with you. I wanted to talk because I don't like the way we left things between us,' he explained, shrugging his shoulders.

Somehow the wounds on his face and lips nearly healed, it was difficult to find traces of the recent beating on his face. The frames of his glasses perfectly masked a small bruise under his eye.

'I see you received your glasses. You look like Jeffrey Dahmer now,' I said sarcastically.

'Like who?' he grimaced, confused.

'Like a Milwaukee cannibal,' I explained with contempt in my voice. 'He was an American serial killer and sex offender who killed and dismembered seventeen men and boys.'

'You have a screw loose, you know that, right?' he grumbled. 'But if that's who I remind you of, you have nothing to fear, you don't look like a boy to me.'

'I didn't choose your frames, you did, pal. It's safe to say that wasn't the greatest choice,' I replied, rather rudely.

This guy triggered my worst instincts. I got off the swing and, still covered in a blanket, walked towards my front door. With a nod of my head, I invited him inside.

From the corner of my eye, I saw a black Mercedes parked next to the gate.

'Did you come here by yourself?'

'Yeah, how else?!'

'Are you coming inside, or are you planning to stand there like a twat?'

'Oh, you're going to get it in a minute, you cheeky cow ...'

'Yeah, yeah ... whatever.' I went inside, leaving the door ajar.

I grabbed my MacBook, a collection of dictionaries, and my mother's diary from the kitchen counter. I swiftly piled them up and placed them on the sideboard.

John strutted in behind me like he owned the place, examining everything in sight. I felt a wave of resentment, knowing how he thought life was his playground. 'I like it here,' he said with approval on his face.

'Thank you, I like it here as well,' I replied with no appreciation for his words.

'Are you going to hiss at me like that all the time?'

'I don't know. It depends on what you have to say to me. Coffee?'

'Yes, please.' He sat down at the table like a well-behaved student, with his hands on his lap, watching all my movements.

I made us some coffee, handed him a cup, and sat across from him.

'I'm all ears, Mr Harris,' I said, looking at him with furrowed brows.

'Well, it's a long, complicated story, kiddo,' he began.

'I think I can manage.'

'Actually, instead of explaining it all to you, maybe it will be better if I show you?' he said after a moment's thought.

'How?'

'I'll take you to one place.'

'Under the pear tree on the left-hand side near the cottage?' I said with a sneer.

He snorted a short laugh.

'You are something else, Lucy. You really are.' He shook his head. 'Go and get dressed, please.'

I was tempted to launch into a witty retort, but my curiosity about what he wanted to show me won. After days spent chained to my desk, editing a novel, I could do with a few hours off.

I left my guest at the table and strutted into the bedroom. I put on a pair of tight jeans and a black jumper, twisted my hair into a loose bun and put on some makeup. It didn't take me long, but John had evidently tired of waiting, as I found him by the bookshelf. He was gripping an old romance in his hands. When he saw me, he snickered sarcastically.

'What a load of crap, cliché after cliché. Listen: *He took the coat off her feminine shoulders.* What other sort of shoulders was he supposed to take it off of?!'

I snorted and rolled my eyes.

'I see that the glasses helped.'

'Yes,' he agreed. 'And by the way, you were right about the mess in my house, I lived like a pig.'

'I know,' I sighed, patting him on the shoulder.

'Ready?'

'Yes. Where are we going?'

'You have to wait and see.'

***

'How did you bruise your knuckles?' I asked in the car, looking at his bruised hands on the steering wheel.

'Never mind how. The most important thing is that I got my car back,' he mocked.

After nearly an hour's drive in his Mercedes, we arrived at an old tenement house, resembling the orphanage described in Frances Hodgson Burnett's novel *The Little Princess*. The richly decorated façade of the building hardly held the front walls, and the windows with scarred glass and rusty bars could fall apart with another gust of wind.

Harris turned off the engine, jumped out of the car, opened my door and presented his hand to help me out.

'Thank you, but I can manage myself,' I said, unmoved by his gesture.

'No doubt, but the lady should be helped.'

'Lady?! Blimey! When did I get an upgrade from cheeky mare to lady?!'

'Quit clowning around,' he said with a wry smile and walked towards the entrance.

Inside, my nostrils were struck by a strange mixture: the pungent smell of detergent and the smell of baby powder. I grimaced.

'You'll get used to it,' he said, seeing the expression on my face. 'Try breathing through your mouth.'

An elderly woman dressed in a work apron appeared in the hallway.

'You got a pass?' she welcomed us with a voice burned by thousands of cigarettes.

'Good morning,' John replied politely. 'Unfortunately, we don't, but I would be very grateful if you could ask Rebecca Lockwood to come and see us, please.'

That said, he grabbed the woman's wrinkled hand to kiss it. She snatched it from him and wiped it on her hip with obvious disgust.

'Name?' she asked unfriendly.

'John Harris, dear lady,' he replied, completely un-deterred.

'Wait here, I'll get her for you.'

'Thank you very much.' John bowed cordially.

I was standing right behind him, slightly stunned by this absurd scene. Harris winked at me and croaked. After a while, we heard the tapping of heels on the tiled floor at the end of the corridor. The footsteps were briskly approaching, and the imagination in my head painted a picture of the Headmistress in the likeness of Miss Trunchbull in the film about Matilda. I was surprised when instead of a stocky woman dressed in an oversized uniform, covered with chocolate cake and wet with students' tears, I saw a petite figure in a white blouse and a black pencil skirt.

When she saw Harris, she stopped stunned by his presence.

'Johnny!' she exclaimed squeakly. 'Is it really you? Or am I dreaming?!'

'Good morning, Becky. Who else!?' he shouted back, opening his arms.

'As I live and breathe!' She jumped up happily, falling into his embrace.

After a few minutes of enthusiastic hugs and shouts, the woman finally realised my presence. She looked questioningly at John.

'It's Lucy,' he said hastily.

She shook her head as if she couldn't believe her eyes.

'Little Lucy Blackbird?!' she asked, staring at me like a rare exhibit.

'In the flesh. Although not so little anymore ...' I replied, equally surprised. 'Sorry, do I know you?'

'Oh, child! You probably don't remember me, how could you!' she said, pulled me close and hugged me. 'I'm so sorry about Maya,' she whispered, and my chest tightened with dread. 'Let's go to the office.'

I followed her, trying to understand what was going on. John looked around the corridor and the rooms he passed along the way.

'Nothing has changed here, has it?' he noticed.

'Well, not much,' Becky admitted with a clear resignation in her voice. 'Everything is falling apart as it has before,' she said opening the office door.

The office was cramped and dreary. Its walls needed fresh, brighter paint, and the furniture desperately needed to be updated. It was clear that the facility we entered had a strict budget. As soon as we stepped in, the woman slammed the door shut and directed us to the two chairs standing against the wall on the other side of her work desk. She perched herself precariously on its edge like a timid bird on the city curb.

'We missed you here, Johnny,' the woman confessed in a tone of complaint. 'Where have you been?'

'I had to take a break from everything, it all got a bit too much, you know ...' he said admittedly and scratched his head in embarrassment. 'Never mind though, how are you holding up? You look great!'

She waved her hand indulgently.

'I'm okay, I guess, I'm holding up purely because I just don't have the time to fall apart,' she said, then sat down in a chair on her side of the desk. 'Are you back for good or is it just a flying visit? Because ...' She nodded in my direction.

'We can talk freely,' he assured her without looking at me. 'Lucy already knows some things, although she doesn't fully realise it yet.'

'Right then, in that case, I have an assignment for you,' she said, reaching into the desk's drawer, she pulled out a large metal box with a number lock and placed it on the desk. She chose a combination of numbers and took out a greenish document folder, identical to the ones I had seen in Harris's cellar.

Seeing it shocked me. I leaned back into the chair and straightened up.

John took the briefcase from her hand and without saying a word put it behind the belt of his trousers at the back.

'I'll call in a few days, we have to go now. The back door code is still the same, right?' he made sure, and when Rebecca confirmed with a short nod, he stood up and kissed her goodbye on the cheek.

He turned towards me and waved his hand at me, encouraging me to leave.

'Not so fast, Harris!' I blurted out, not moving from my place. I rebelliously crossed my arms over my chest. 'I have a few questions. To begin with, tell me how she knew my mother?'

Rebecca and John exchanged faint smiles. The woman opened another drawer. She stared at its contents for a moment as if wondering how much she should explain to me, and then shifted her gaze to me.

'You know where you are, don't you?' she asked as if the answer was obvious.

'And how am I supposed to know that?!' I grumbled, suddenly annoyed by the whole situation.

'Relax, birdy,' said the woman with a tender tone in her voice.

'Excuse me?! Only my mother called me that. How did you ...'

'Oh, there it is!' she interrupted me, finished searching the drawer and placed the blue envelope on the top of the desk, and moved it towards me. 'There you have it. Enough mysteries.'

With trembling fingers, I pulled out a piece of black cardboard from the envelope. It bore the inscription 'Refuge, 1998.'

'What sort of Refuge is it?' I asked, not understanding what I was looking at.

'Turn it around.'

On the other side of the cardboard was a photo of two women and a child.

'The one on the left is me, then your mum and you, Lucy. You lived here for a while, honey. You were around three years old then,' she explained, leaning again on the edge of the desk next to me. 'Refuge is a charity providing specialist support for women and children experiencing domestic violence,' she explained.

'I don't understand ...' I said, completely confused. 'Were we homeless?'

'No, no.' She shook her head firmly. 'Maya worked here as a support worker. And because commuting was burdensome for her, and she had a constant problem with arranging babysitting for you, you both lived here for some time, in one of our annexes. That's how I know who you are and how we used to call you.'

'There you have it, kiddo. All clear,' Harris interjected impatiently. 'Can we go now?'

'No!' I said and turned my head round towards Rebecca. 'So, were you friends with my mum then?' I asked.

'We had a tight bond for almost three years, working our shifts side by side. But then fate gave her the chance to realise her childhood dream of joining a library—and we needed to loosen our ties. We still kept in touch though, until ... now,' she pouted sadly. 'I'm kicking myself that I only found out about her funeral recently. I can't believe that after all we had been through together, I missed our last goodbye.'

'I'm sorry, but ...' I spread my hands in a gesture of helplessness. 'I let everyone know about the funeral, but it turns out my mother knew people who I had no idea existed ...'

The woman nodded in understanding.

'Lucy, please, let's go!' urged John. 'It's about lunch-time. I have to get out of here before the women can see me ... Becky, please back me up on this!'

'Johnny is right,' she confirmed. 'Men are not welcome here. They cause unnecessary stress in the residents, and we try to protect them from it.'

'I see,' I said, hurriedly rising from my chair.

'Keep the picture, birdy!' the woman protested when I wanted to give her the photograph back. 'I have a few more of these at home. You keep this one as a keepsake,' she said and gave me another warm hug. I didn't even realise how much I missed hugs.

'Can I come here again, please?' I whispered.

'Of course!' she replied, pushing me arms-length away to give John a knowing look. 'Something tells me that we will see each other sooner than you think ...'

'That said ... we have to go, now!' the man grumbled nervously, looking out the slightly ajar door into the hall-way. 'Last call, kid. Come on! Becks, expect me in a few days.'

'Thank you very much,' she said warmly, kissing him on the cheek.

'I'll bring a few pennies … It's been a while since I gave you anything.'

We said goodbye quickly and ran towards the back exit. He punched the code into the digital lock and slammed the door behind us.

'Phew!' he sighed with relief in his voice.

'How bad would it be if they saw you there?'

'Quite bad, kid. Especially if I'd stumbled across a fresh resident. You know, right after the assault.'

'I understand.'

'These women are mentally shattered. Wounds on their bodies heal much faster than those in their heads. You have to give them as much time and space as possible …' he said it so softly that my heart warmed.

I couldn't deny the spike of envy that surged through me when I witnessed the undeniable bond between Harris and Rebecca. I was ready to bombard him with a million questions. I just had to wait for the right moment. But as soon as I settled into his car, my demeanour softened. It seemed that Harris had a soft side after all. 'I'm a bit hungry. How about you?' I asked instead.

'Well, I could demolish a burger or something. What do you fancy?'

'I don't know. Let's drive home and see what we can find on the way …?'

'Fresh roadkill?' he laughed.

'Yes, a badger à la tripe on the road.'

'Mmm, delicious, count me in! Do you want to go home, or would you rather let me show you what

I wanted and explain?' he asked, turning the key in the ignition.

'I'd rather go home,' I replied after a moment of hesitation. 'I need to work for a bit ... I'll come and visit you after the weekend.'

'You are not planning to work on Saturday, are you?' he said surprised. 'Weekends are for relaxing, not working! Even your workaholic mother used to say so.'

'True.'

'So? Let's go back to yours to grab some of your things for the weekend away. And tomorrow, I'll tell you everything you want to know, agreed?'

'Agreed.'

'It didn't take long to persuade you,' he said, smirking.

'You got me ... I'm too curious about what you're hiding to want to wait any longer than I have to, I guess. On the other hand, I'm afraid of what you have to say to me. Because once I know, there will probably be no turning back, right?'

'I think the picture you paint in your head about this whole cellar situation is much more colourful than it really is, kiddo.'

I sighed. 'That remains to be seen.'

A good old British burger and coffee from the burger van satisfied our moderately refined taste buds. We went back to my house, I packed some clothes and toiletries, and afterwards, we left to go to John's cottage. On the way, we settled for a comfortable silence that suited both of us very well.

We arrived in the early evening. Harris lit a fire, the flames flickered into existence and the warmth of that old fireplace slowly crawled across the room. For a moment, I was lost in the dance of those flames, it took a moment or two to break myself free and into the kitchen to prepare dinner and brew a pot of tea for us both. After the meal, he went outside and started to stock up chopped logs, and I buried myself under the blanket and carried on reading Celie's adventures from *The Colour Purple* while Julian the cat curled up at my feet.

It was a nice evening. John and I gave ourselves some respite and space before the next day. The day that was supposed to bring answers to the burning questions inside of me.

Sunday, 2 October

'Time to get up, sleepy head. You said you had trouble sleeping, but you snored like a trooper most of the night,' he said, tapping me on the shoulder.

I rubbed my eyes and sat on the bed. The clock on the wall struck eight a.m. The room smelled of freshly brewed coffee. Julian purred, emptying his bowl.

'Seriously? Was I snoring? I'm sorry,' I said half-heartedly.

John shrugged his shoulders and went outside. After a while, he came back in and said:

'My spade has gone missing!'

'What spade?'

He scratched his head with a thoughtful look on his face as if trying hard to help create a memory portrait. 'An old, rusty spade with a wooden handle, which was leaning against the wall of the shed since I can remember ... And now it's gone.'

'Ah, that spade!' I whispered in a sudden dazzle. 'It's under the bed ...'

He looked at me with a furrowed brow, then knelt and looked under the bed.

'How did it get there?' he gasped after a moment.

'I used it to break the padlock ...' I replied with embarrassment in my voice.

'Uuu, MacGyver!' he laughed.

'Necessity is the mother of invention,' I said with relief, smiling back. 'Why do you need this spade now anyway?'

'I have to dig the corpse out from under the pear tree,' he said seriously. He put on a khaki hooded jacket and went outside.

I jumped out of bed and chased after him. Indeed, he stood under the pear tree.

'You must be joking!' I said, chattering my teeth in the autumn cold. 'John!'

'John, John ...' he grumbled, then stood up with his back to the trunk of the tree.

I watched in bewilderment as he measured three steps to the left and then drove his spade into the grassy ground.

'Go and get dressed,' he said, looking at me with disapproval. 'People will start talking if someone sees you walking around here in your pjs.'

'All of a sudden, you started to care what people think?!' I replied in disbelief.

'I don't care,' he explained. 'But it will be much better for us if we don't draw too much attention to ourselves.'

'We?'

'Well, willy-nilly, after today you will become one of us,' he said enigmatically and continued digging. 'Please, go back in and get dressed.'

'No way, I want to see this corpse first.'

'You are as sharp as a bowling ball, sometimes.' He laughed. 'Please, go inside and I'll bring what I dig up inside.'

'That's not an option!' I declared categorically, wrapping my arms around myself. 'Carry on digging, Harris!'

John hurled another spade load of dirt to the side and as he dug into the ground once more, we both heard the distinct sound of hitting something metallic signalling the success of the morning's excavations.

He then knelt and began to shovel the ground with his hands. I couldn't see what was in the hole, so I stepped forward a little. He had already opened the lid of the blue metal box. I opened my mouth in amazement.

'Catch,' he said, throwing the rolled-up bills into my hands.

I waited for some explanation, but my companion closed the chest and began to push the soil from the side into the hole. 'Go back inside now. I'm serious, Lucy!'

In an act of encouragement, he slapped me on the butt with the spade.

This time I obeyed, clutching the bills in my hand. John was right, I shouldn't look conspicuous, especially near a valuable stash! Before I entered the house, I looked around carefully. As if that could change anything! My conspiracy was really pathetic, and I grimaced in embarrassment.

***

I was combing my hair, frantically wondering what I had accidentally got myself into when red-faced Harris entered the house. He poured himself a glass of water from the tap and drank it greedily.

'I've never liked digging,' he murmured. 'I thought my heart was about to pop out at some point.'

'Do you want a coffee?' I asked, tying my hair with an elastic band.

'No, thanks, I had one not long ago,' he replied, settling down heavily in his chair.

I made myself a cup of tea and gave him another glass of water. Then I moved a chair near him and said:

'Question number one. What sort of money is this, and where did it come from?'

He shrugged.

'It's money from the sales of my books. I get a royalty from the publishing house every three months,' he replied in a tone as if it were the most obvious thing in the world.

I whistled in amazement. I had been working in the publishing industry for several years, and I knew that authors rarely earned any big sums. Looking at the wad of banknotes, one thing was for sure—Harris must have been doing quite well. He must be an extremely popular author! Unless he lied and the money came from a different source ...

He must have noticed my disbelief because he added:

'Strangely enough, people still read my books. And believe it or not, some of them still appear on the best-sellers lists in the UK and US.'

I still had my doubts.

'Then why haven't I read anything of yours yet?!'

He spread his hands and then croaked.

'I bet you did, kid. My books are in bookstores all over England and the US. You just don't realise that it is me writing them, as I use an alias.'

I couldn't figure out whether he was screwing with me or not, so I changed the subject just in case.

'Would it not be easier to keep the money in a bank?!' I asked.

'Maybe, but I prefer to keep it under the pear tree. This way I always have cash readily available. Question number two?'

'Just tell me everything!' I demanded.

'Okay,' he agreed. 'Which version of events do you want: detailed or shortened?'

'The one with the smallest details, obviously.'

'You may regret this decision, I am warning you,' he said with a mischievous grin. He sat down in his chair and clasped his hands in front of him. 'It all started in the summer of ninety-six. Maya was working with Becky at the Refuge for several weeks ...'

'Right, and?'

'Don't interrupt me!' he snapped impatiently. 'Everything I'm saying is important and if you break my concentration, I'll be sure to miss something.' His voice had a sharp edge that cut through the air. 'Well, that summer Maya came to visit us, that is, Laura and me, with you, for the weekend. She was very uneasy and clearly broken inside, but she did not want to admit what was bothering her. Laura had to use some girl tricks to finally squeeze some truths out of her ... As you can imagine, it wasn't easy for your mum to work amongst victims of violence. After all, the women in the centre had very similar experiences to hers. She said that as long as she didn't come in contact with other women who had been harmed in relationships, the whole Luke thing healed over, and she had no intention of re-opening the healed wounds. She came to terms with what had happened, because she knew that despite the tragedy, you both had a chance for a normal life. You,' he pointed at me, 'had perfect conditions to develop properly. Her many horrific recollections and a sensation of immense hurt were awoken only by the sight of battered mothers holding their children in their arms, pleading for help from the staff at all hours of the day or night.'

'That was stupid of her, wasn't it,' I said, shrugging my shoulders.

'What was?' he asked surprised by my words.

'Why did my mother even start working there?! After all, she knew what kind of women were sent to such places!'

'Lucy, I didn't suspect you to be so shallow. Anyway, I told you not to interrupt me!'

'Me? Shallow?!' I was outraged.

'After all, Maya took this job because there was not much work available at that time near where you both lived. Do you think it was easy to find a job in your small town? Especially with a little child? You should really learn to bite your tongue sometimes, kiddo,' he snapped at me, frowning. 'The fact was that this job gave Maya and you, for that matter, enough money to pay for what you needed, but mentally it did not do her any good. With each week she worked there, she fell into a deeper depression, she stopped dealing with her emotions. Laura and I decided to get her out of there. My wife even felt guilty because she found out about the vacancy from Becky ... Laura and Becky were sisters, have I mentioned it before? Maya didn't want to hear about quitting. She insisted that she would stay there and continue to help those women. She also said that she would eventually get used to it all, that she would toughen up, and that she was not going to feel sorry for herself,' he said, sighing.

'That all sounds very noble,' I interjected sceptically. 'But what could she do on her own?'

'On her own? ... Not much,' he admitted, smiling mysteriously. 'But as they say: in life, it is not important what you know but who you know, right? At first, we thought that Maya was tripping a little and as soon as she sees that she is not able to do too much, she will let go and leave by her choice. But you know what your mum was like ... She was stubborn like a mule. After some time, she invited us to the Refuge house. That's when we met Martin.'

'Martin?'

'At the time, Becky's new boyfriend. We quickly became friends because it turned out that we were on the same page.'

'Meaning?'

John sat in silence as if trying to find the right way to describe it, but no words came to him. He scratched his neck, got up from his chair, and took a box of cigars from the drawer of his dresser. He plucked one, bit off the tip, and threw it into the fireplace. Finally, he lit it, and for a few seconds, his face disappeared in a cloud of smoke.

'You know,' he said, sitting back in his chair. 'Somehow all five of us just clicked as if we had known each other forever. We spent two days in Martin's flat nearby. He worked as an accountant at the shelter alongside Becky and Maya, but sometimes, when it was necessary, he helped as a security man. We quickly learnt that, despite the efforts of the staff, there was a lot that had to be done for these women. The aid scheme felt like a sham. These poor women had no guarantees and no hope of long-term improvement, and their abusers knew exactly where to find them. They would invade them in the centre, dangling false promises of improvement in front of them; others threatened them; some even managed to inflict violence again, others kidnapped their kids in an attempt to force their woman back to their home, playing mind games of where they belong, they would do anything to get back that control. The situation seemed hopeless.'

'I can only imagine,' I interjected.

'Just then, after almost an all-night debate over drinks, a plan was born to help these women in a bit of a different way. We knew that we couldn't do much in conventional ways, so we decided to take things into our own hands ...'

'And?!' I asked, very intrigued, and moved to the edge of my seat.

'And we did, kiddo. And we did ... You must know that when you meet these women, even for a moment, you find yourself surging with some extreme emotions. You quickly realise how many degenerates without principles, or any moral backbones live around us.' He waved his hand angrily. 'The picture of fear in these women's eyes doesn't leave you alone ... It soaks into your skin like a stench and stays with you for a very long time.'

'Well, so what plan did you all come up with then?!' I asked impatiently.

'We decided to use all the resources we had and help them. We literally felt the support of some higher power ... Becky and Maya collected information about the psychos, you know, names, surnames, addresses, etc. It took a while because we had to have as much detail as possible. It was necessary to know who we were facing in order to help effectively. Every case was unique in its own way. I heard stories of women who had been imprisoned by their partners and desperately needed to find family members to take them in. It was a classic case of coercive control: these abusers wanted the women to be isolated from their friends and family so that they could keep their control over them. For others, we tried to figure out what kind of work and childcare options were suitable for them. Thankfully, through Laura's work at the Job Centre, she knew first-hand of any jobs as soon as they became available, which made things easier. Although she was doing her best to help, I knew that I had to put in extra effort if I wanted to make a real difference.'

'That's very noble of you ...'

'Problems arose when work and new accommodation weren't enough. You must know that quite a large percentage of these women suffer from Stockholm syndrome ...'

'Yes, I read about it once ... The long-term victim of violence no longer defended herself against her abuser, she simply flattened her spine to the wall and stayed out of sight. She felt a strange pull of empathy for him despite his despicable actions. Someone like her was too broken and started to feel responsible for all the violence. Victims have an uncanny ability to convince themselves their tormentors couldn't help it—the angry outbursts were all their fault.'

'Exactly. It's like a psychological addiction ... A terrible thing. For a while, the victims leave the abusers and then they go back. They often speak about them in superlatives, point out their strengths, ignoring the harm they have done to them. In closer contact, it turns out that they completely subordinated to their partner, stopped thinking independently ... It's such a vicious circle.'

'Horrible thing to experience.'

'Indeed,' he agreed. Furthermore, children and the lack of money come to the picture, as men earn more and make women dependent on them not only psychologically but also financially. Clever bustards. Most of these wankers are just regular folk, with regular jobs and seemingly normal lives. Everyone at work admires them for their intellect, wit and ambition—but behind closed doors, there is a different story: they possess a darker side. Whether it be a vet, or a CEO of a major tech firm, these execrable individuals inflict immense anguish on their victims in secret, taking pleasure in their horrifying deeds.'

'Shit wrapped in golden paper.'

'Women in that sort of abuse are the hardest to help. Cutting them off from such a detrimental partner would be their only means of salvation—it's an arduous task, yet one that must be achieved.'

John was watching me closely, probably trying to read my face if I had already guessed what he would say next.

'And? Did you manage to get rid of them?' I asked, afraid of the answer.

'Yeah,' he said.

'How?!'

'For good. How else?!' he laughed pitifully.

'Fucking hell!' I grabbed my head. 'You mean all those men in the pictures in your cellar ... They are all dead?'

'Have you completely lost your mind?' he got irritated. 'Are you even listening to what I'm saying to you?'

'Well, I'm listening. That's why I'm asking!'

'I explained that most cases were limited to getting a job or finding relatives. The files were created for all the cases,' he said irritably.

'What about the rest?'

'Oh, for fuck's sake with you!' he shouted, rose from his chair and walked outside, slamming the door.

I sat stunned by his reaction for a while, glancing at the roll of money on the table. *Where did it really come from?* Had he intended to give the money to Becky, or was he planning to give it to me in exchange for my silence? If so, why would he tell me all this? It didn't make sense at all ...

I heard the clash of metal against wood and rushed to the garden. I hesitantly pushed open the shed door, and there he was—Harris, his trusty axe flying through the air like an extension of his arm. His face was intense with fury as he chopped away at logs like a man possessed. 'I guess every stump has my face on it, huh?' I said jokingly.

'Almost.'

'Should I leave?'

He sighed draughtily, freezing with his axe raised above his head.

'No. You should get a grip,' he said dryly. 'You've been irritating me since you woke up. What got into you today?'

'I don't understand why you are so pissed off with me! Just because I asked a few questions?' I murmured. 'After all, any normal person would ...'

'I asked you to stop interrupting while I was trying to tell you everything,' he gasped, going back to chopping the logs. 'It was all very serious matters ... not some chit-chat with mates over coffee!'

He was furious. He must have regretted everything he said to me. I felt like a child being told off in the principal's office.

'I'm sorry,' I whispered.

I felt like crying. What a pity I didn't come here in my car! I would have already left. Without giving it a second thought, I headed towards the road leading to the village.

'Where are you going?' he yelled after me.

'Home!' I hissed because I didn't like his tone. What was he thinking ...?!

'Good luck with that! Great plan, kid! A hundred and fifty-mile-walk in slippers! Brilliant! Very wise,' he added mockingly.

I turned around angrily. Realising that I really didn't even think it through. Harris drove an axe into a large stump on which he was splitting smaller bits of wood.

'Come on, you plonker,' he said resignedly and waved his hand towards the house.

I followed him, knowing that I wouldn't have got far without my wallet, phone, and shoes.

I stood in the doorway, watching him packing some things in his backpack. Then he put on his jacket and baseball cap and reached out without a word to me with a grey hoodie in his hand.

'Put it on, so you don't get cold out there,' he said, tapping me on the shoulder.

'Where would I get ...?'

'You are asking too many questions, Miss Blackbird. Sometimes you just have to shut up and let others speak,' he said.

I was about to reply but then he smiled warmly. I followed him towards the shed where he disappeared for a while and then came out, holding two oars in his hands. He handed me one of them and smiled again. I frowned, not too thrilled with his idea.

'Seriously?!' I groaned.

'Yeah. Come on.'

We strolled along the path, our feet treading with familiarity as we neared the lake. I felt a chill in the air as we approached the edge of the lake and saw the rowboat lying on its back in the tall grass.

John turned it over and slid it into the water without much effort. He sat down on the back bench, put the backpack at his feet, and fixed the paddle in the handle on the side. I handed him the second oar, and then he pointed his hand to the bench in the middle. I staggered onto the boat looking around for the life jacket. I couldn't swim very well and the vision of landing in cold water without a vest seemed unpleasant, to say the least.

'Don't be afraid,' he murmured, seeing the concern on my face. 'You won't fall. Unless you deliberately want to jump in.'

It made him laugh because he croaked.

'I don't plan to go swimming today.'

'Then sit down and relax a little, kid. Look around you, take it all in. Look at all these beautiful colours here!'

'Indeed, autumn has painted beautiful scenery this year ...' I whispered, looking at the colourful crowns of the trees.

John took a deep breath and grabbed the oars.

The sunlight rays broke through the blanket of white clouds, lighting up the still surface of the lake like a mirror. He rowed steadily and the boat glided forward, leaving behind a trail of tranquillity. He seemed lost in thought, his face painted with peace he probably hadn't felt for a while. Maybe it was Laura he was thinking about. I rested both hands on the bench and tilted my head up to the sun, closing my eyes as I soaked in every second of this quintessential autumn day; the warmth from its rays embracing me with comfort while a gentle breeze kissed my cheeks.

'Isn't it funny how you can get so lost in life?' John said, pulling me away from the gentle rocking. 'You fall for someone's idealised vision of themselves but when reality sets in ... well, that person's true colours can be a bit disappointing. It's such a shame, isn't it?' His voice trailed off into nothingness.

I didn't quite understand the message, but I bit my lip. I wanted to ask what he meant but I knew any further questioning would only annoy him.

'Laura and Becky's old man had a similar MO to those chaps who were in the files. His wife took off when they were eight and ten respectively. Nobody knows if she left him, or if something else happened and she just vanished. They were then looked after by their grandma until she passed away and there was no one to keep their father in line. He started having a go at them when he was tanked up. It went on for the best part of a few years ... Until eventually he drank himself into an early grave, and the girls could finally lead proper lives together.'

Everything was slowly starting to fall into place.

'Both girls went on to Uni, Becky took sociology, Laura did admin,' he continued. 'At the beginning of the first year, she burst into the classroom late, walked like a hurricane past my bench and sat in the row in front of me. Her long auburn curls smelt of rain and wind, which, combined with the smell of her perfume, made my pants tight immediately,' he laughed. 'What can I say? I was besotted at first sight. She wasn't too keen on me straight away. Many years later, she told me that she'd judged me harshly for having a fit physique and thinking I was an arrogant show-off.'

I smiled.

'Lucky for me, we had to do a bit of practical work together, and we started spending more time with each other after classes. It took some effort but eventually, I got Laura to fall for me. Mind you, she had been through the wringer emotionally. I had to be very careful and gentle. Through it all, I found out I had it in me to win her over. Thank heavens, she gave her heart to me—and I looked after it right up until its last beat ...'

The boat jolted to a stop, my heart tightening into the lump that was growing bigger and bigger in my throat. I twisted around on the bench to face him. His baseball cap was hanging low over his eyes, but I could tell he had been weeping. This man, who moments before had told me such an intimate tale of sorrowful longing for his wife, seemed to be completely crushed by his emotions. I knew it was up to me to break the silence so I uttered quietly, 'Can I row for a bit, please?'

'Do you know how to?'

'No,' I admitted with a laugh. The boat rocked under the influence of my movements. 'It can't be that hard to learn, if you can do it, so can I. Besides, we are in the middle of the lake, so the chances of hitting anything are thin. Don't you think?'

'All right, smarty pants,' he said. I managed to make him laugh. 'Let's switch places for a moment ... But remember, as soon as you start being silly with it, I will take the oars off you.'

'I'm not twelve!' I said, strumming astern.

'True, by the way, how old are you again?'

'I've told you before, don't you remember?'

He grumbled.

'No. So maybe you will kindly remind me?'

'I'll be twenty-eight in March.'

'Oh yeah, I remember now,' he replied, reaching for his backpack and unfastening the zipper of one of the compartments. 'Do you want a drink?'

I somehow was not surprised that his backpack had a place for a bottle of whiskey and glasses.

'Do you have Coke and ice?' I asked wickedly.

'At your age, you should be drinking it without a Coke, kid ...'

Although not so complex, the art of rowing, was certainly no easy task. I had been pulling on the oars for what felt like hours but could have been only minutes, and my arms were already screaming in protest. On the opposite side of the boat, John casually sipped away at his whiskey whilst smoking a cigar. He seemed pleasantly content with this heinous jaunt. I gritted my teeth and ignored my burning muscles, vowing to show him that this seemingly never-ending voyage would not break me. Harris gave me a knowing smirk from time to time, almost as if he was sorry for me.

'Tell me something about yourself,' I said, trying to hide the gasping in my voice. 'Who were your parents?'

'It's going to be a short story, Lucy. I never knew my folks. I grew up in an orphanage. As soon as I came of age, I went to work and moved out to live on my own. The orphanage helped me find a small flat. I somehow finished my studies, married Laura ... I worked in construction for the best part of three decades before finally calling it a day. I was good at what I did. In my spare time, I wrote books ... And that's pretty much it.'

'Let's not forget one more hobby of yours,' I interjected.

'I wouldn't call it a hobby,' he said in such a tone as if he wanted to dismiss me. 'I don't want to go into insignificant details with you. The most important thing is that you understand why we did what we did. And that's it.'

'I understand what drove you,' I assured him hastily. 'But I still have a lot of questions ...'

'For example?'

'For example, what happened with your car, where did you disappear to that morning, and who were these men who took you for *a ride*?' I let the paddles out of my hand for a second and put my fingers in quotation marks. 'And how did they know where to look for you? You have said before that no one knew where you were hiding. And what did you mean when you said it was my fault that they were able to find you?'

Harris blinked, stunned by the avalanche of questions.

'Okay. Let's just say that ...'

'Not "let's just say"!' I was irritated. 'I want to know the truth if you think it was my fault.'

He sighed and began to rummage through his backpack again.

'I'm hungry. How about you?'

'Don't change the subject!'

'I'm thinking roast chicken and vegetables.'

'Oh, for God's sake!'

'It's gone cold, don't you think?' he said, then drank the rest of his whiskey and ordered, 'Let's go back! Swap seats with me because with your rowing pace, we won't get to the shore by sunset. I'll have the oars back, please.'

Every day, every single infernal hour, he managed to make my blood boil with his self-righteous shtick. I threw the oars on the boat's floor with a loud thud and dramatically sank into the middle bench, turning my back to him in a clear display of defiance. Instead of telling me everything in one fell swoop, he liked to build up the tension and spoon-feed me the facts.

Suddenly, an ingenious plan came to me—it was time to take matters into my own hands and discover everything there was to know. A wicked plot quickly formed in my mind. When we reached the shore, I jumped out of the boat quickly and headed towards the path leading to his house.

'Chicken and vegetables, right?' I called innocently, already on the slope.

He looked at me a little dismayed. He was just about to pull the boat ashore. I knew it would take him a while.

'Yes, please,' he replied.

'I'll see what's in the fridge,' I said with a smile. 'If we need anything, I'll pop down the shop, okay?'

'Yeah, yeah, no worries.'

'Can I take your car? I don't feel like walking.'

'No problem, the keys should be next to the cigar box on the dresser.'

I already knew where he kept the spare key to the house, so I ran through the woods. At home, for peace of mind, I looked in the fridge and the vegetable basket. To be honest, I could use the products I had at hand to prepare the meal, but I had to get out of the house to put my plan in place.

As I put my seatbelt on, John appeared from the edge of the forest. I waved nonchalantly and sped off towards the village shop.

When I entered, a chatty saleswoman bombarded me with inquiries about Harris. Annoyed and eager to shake her off, I feigned a work call on my mobile. While browsing aimlessly with a basket in hand, she cast knowing glances in my direction. 'Thank you and goodbye,' I said.

'Ta-ta!' she replied with saccharine condescension. 'Just for future reference, love, you would do best to remember that we don't get signal down here in the shop ...'

I rolled my eyes at my own foolishness. Once I was out of there, I checked my phone and sure enough, I had no bars whatsoever. So, I got in the car, threw my mobile on the passenger seat, and drove off towards the church on top of the hill, hoping to catch a signal. My plan of action paid off as it turned out—I started to hear some message beeps near the entrance gates. Parking the car up by the bench overlooking John's lake, I finally reconnected with the world. From the hill, I could just about see the cottage tucked away amongst all those trees ... And there was a tell-tale wisp of smoke wafting from its chimney. I dialled my GP's number with a sigh. I was very aware of the time constraints before Harris would start to suspect something was fishy, so I was very direct and to the point in my conversation. Doctor Patel wasn't one to question me, which suited me fine. I was fully aware that his drinking habit had numbed his senses and made him more lenient towards me—something I would never admit out loud. After a few minutes, an email pinged through with the attachment I needed. When I checked the location of the nearest pharmacy, I smiled inwardly at the short distance I had to travel. Another lucky break.

The pharmacist pouted her cherry-red lips as she tapped away at the keyboard, entering the code to my e-prescription. She examined me from head to toe through thick layers of powdery blue eye shadow before snidely asking if work was stressful. 'Something like that,' I replied coolly, not wanting to complicate things with the gruelling details. While she busied herself with my prescription, I couldn't help but examine her gaudy attire and wonder what she could possibly be trying to prove.

'You are lucky we are open on Sundays. And we are about to close, in six minutes exactly. So pure luck, I say.'

'Oh, yes, lucky me!' I replied enthusiastically, barely hiding the mockery. 'Great gratitude fills my heart that I managed to get here just before closing!'

The pharmacist gave me a nonchalant look. She looked like she was fond of showing customers that she was doing them a massive favour by her mere presence in the pharmacy.

'The medicine should be taken orally,' she grumbled.

'I guessed it wasn't supposed to be done rectally,' I said sweetly. 'Thank you and goodbye!'

I got in my car, pulled the pills out of the packet, then pressed my phone against the dashboard, I crushed the four tablets—enough to get my plan formalised effectively. Slipping the powder into the pharmacy receipt, I stored it in my pocket and threw the empty packet in the glove compartment.

After arriving back at the cottage, I stepped out of the car and straightened my posture with a deep exhale. Wiping my clammy hands on my trousers, I made my way towards the entrance—only to find Harris perched by the fireplace, engrossed in a book. His gaze shifted upwards as soon as he heard me approach, his lips curling into a reassured smile as he took the plastic bags from my shaking hands.

'Come on, kid, what did you get?' he asked with uncharacteristic tenderness. 'I've already prepared everything. Let me just cut some veg and I'll chuck it all in the oven.'

I smiled, slipped my hand into my pocket, and squeezed the receipt. It burned my fingers with a guilty fire, in which I would probably have to fry after death for what I was about to do to him.

'I've never seen you so quiet, what's got into you?' he said with concerned curiosity.

'It's nothing,' I responded before sprinting to the loo.

Once I was in front of the mirror, I stared at my reflection. I could not believe what I was about to do. But I knew I had to follow my instinct, so I could finally make sense of this mess and get some closure.

The aromas from John's cooking filled my nostrils as I re-entered the living room area. The warmth radiating from the fireplace seemed to hug me like an old friend. I kicked off my boots and peeled off my hoodie, leaving it on top of my handbag. John hummed as he busied himself in the kitchen. I suspected he enjoyed cooking. I caught myself smiling at him despite what I was about to do to him. There was nothing for me to prepare, so instead I started picking at the chipped polish on my nails, daydreaming about what this night would bring.

'Coffee with Baileys?' asked Harris directly into my ear and handed me the steaming cup. 'I'm glad that you bought some alcohol, kid. Dinner is almost ready. Could you get the plates and cutlery, please?'

'Sure,' I replied and went to the kitchen as asked.

John sat by the table and sipped on his Irish coffee, then pulled the food out of the oven and dished on to the plates. We sat down at the table. I was hungry and nervous, so I stuffed my face with vegetables and chicken like a savage.

'Enjoying your meal, I see?!' he said mockingly.

'Mmm,' I mumbled with my mouth full. 'Cheers.'

'Drink up, or you'll get hiccups!' he laughed.

I listened. I took a big sip of hot coffee that wrapped around my throat, and the alcohol soon brought relaxation.

Monday, 3 October

My tongue felt like sandpaper, a metallic taste coating the inside of my mouth. I tried to move my face, but it felt like lead. I was lying in bed, and I could see the familiar crack on the ceiling above me. My eyes widened when I started to process the images of the surroundings before me. I squinted, then slowly pushed myself up on my elbows. Something wasn't right. The dresser should be there, near the table with Julian playing by the fireplace and John snoring on the recliner chair. But nothing looked as I'd expected.

I twitched when I realised that I was in the bedroom of my family home instead of the cottage.

'What the hell?!'

My mind was foggy—I had to pause and take a deep breath every few seconds. My head felt like it had been subject to an underwater explosion as if all the memories that were stored inside my brain had instantly vanished from existence. The pain was so intense that I could barely move. I had no other choice but to lay there motionless for a moment and try to subdue it. I subconsciously ran my hands along the crumpled sheets, propped a pillow under my back, and peered at my dull reflection in the mirror. As far as clothing went, I was still wearing yesterday's T-shirt and jeans, which seemed to be a total mismatch with the present situation I found myself in.

And then something caught my eye. A scruffy piece of paper wedged between the nightstand and the wall—it was ripped out from one of the notebooks which I typically used when writing down random ideas or musings. That MUST have been what triggered this bizarre episode of mine.

Have you actually lost your bloody mind?! Pentothal? What were you thinking, kid?! What did you want to do with it, hah? I thought you were smarter than that! I hope you like the taste of your own medicine! I left the front door key under the doormat. Don't bother getting back in contact with me. Goodbye.

I entered the bathroom, swaying slightly. I barely had enough energy to push the door open, and when I saw my reflection in the mirror, I almost fainted. My face had a ghoulish pallor, bloodshot eyes reminiscent of a vampire from an old storybook, and deep shadows pooled under my eyes. The wave of nausea hit me like a fist, and I quickly lunged for the porcelain toilet bowl. Another spasm wracked my body as I heaved and retched until there was nothing left inside me. Chills travelled up and

down my spine and icy sweat soaked through my clothes as I lay on the floor, struggling to regain control of my leaden limbs. After a few agonising minutes, I managed to drag myself upright and gulped down several mouthfuls of cold water from the tap. Catching sight of my reflection once more, I splashed some water on my face before stumbling out of the bathroom.

I went back to my room and read the message again. I felt like an idiot. It dawned on me that I really didn't think it all through. But I still didn't understand how he managed to see through me so quickly. One thing was for sure I missed the chance to get any answers and I killed the trust that slowly began to build between us.

I went downstairs, turned the lock on the front door, and took the key out from under the doormat. As I leaned over, my head started to spin again.

My mind flashed with the idea of calling Harris to say sorry. But I was so embarrassed that I couldn't get the words out. Yet, he did it to me purposely, so it didn't seem worth apologising.

I was humiliated but my rage began smouldering in my belly like a fire being stoked. I decided to embrace the fact that mum's wish list would never be fulfilled.

I had a sneaking suspicion that this quest would be more trouble than it was worth. His secrets seemed to stretch out for miles, and the pieces of information I managed to uncover were not ones I could just blab about over brunch with my mates.

I would wager even my mum couldn't have predicted what kind of trouble I'd find myself in when she asked me to do this favour for her. After all, no story was exciting enough to justify getting caught up in the dark web of memories from years past.

My insides churned as I managed to stomach my barely touched toast and lukewarm coffee. I was determined to take my mind off the drama of yesterday, so plonked myself down on the sofa with my laptop and a cozy blanket. Scanning the novel sent by the publishing house, it felt like I'd stepped into a mess; typos galore, yawn-inducing scenes and boring characters. This would take my utmost commitment to sort out.

Only the twilight in the room and stiffness from cold fingers made me realise that I had spent several hours working. I turned on the heating and then the lamp on the table by the armrest of the couch. I stretched and shook my head, trying to relax my stiff neck. Furthermore, I brewed a pot of tea with lots of ginger and lemon. I believed it would do me good.

I looked into my e-mail box, where a message from the editor-in-chief was waiting for me. He informed me of an upcoming meeting approving the publishing plan for the next calendar year.

I was worried and nervous. The thought of seeing Josh again sent my stomach into somersaults. We had a brief fling, and it almost cost me my job. Our attraction started innocently, and conversations about work slowly turned flirtatious. We soon realised that something more was at play between us—we were drawn to each other like moths to a flame. The adrenaline of sneaking around the office, trying not to be caught only inflamed our desire further. We couldn't keep our hands off each other, but I never guessed he was in an actual relationship with an older woman. His naivety didn't stop us from indulging in our passionate affair and risking it all for each other.

The flame went out one sultry evening when the CEO caught us red-handed in one of the offices. He threatened to tell Josh's partner, who was a good friend of his wife. I do not know how exactly Josh managed to alleviate the situation, but there were no major problems. After a short and substantive conversation, fearing for our jobs, we decided to change our relationship to a purely professional one.

Immediately after these events, I received a company laptop, which enabled me to work remotely. My visits to the office became very sporadic. At that time, working from home was very convenient for me because my mother had just received a terrible diagnosis, and I could give her maximum attention.

Several people from work came to the funeral, including the CEO. He told me to take a few days off to get myself together. He added that he saw no contraindications for me to work remotely full-time but not to hesitate to come to the office any time. I realised then, that thanks to my reliable work, I managed to redeem myself for a setback with Josh, and I was on the right track to buy into the good graces of the boss again.

Josh's message was the first request for a meeting since mum's death. I accepted the invitation and after a while, I received an email with details: date, place, and time. I breathed a sigh of relief. I had twelve days to prepare myself mentally for seeing them all once more.

Friday, 14 October

The conference room was spacious, the office was teeming with life, filled with lively conversations of the publishing house's employees who, like me, had arrived to take part in the annual budget meeting.

From the moment I entered the building, I was flooded with a stream of condolences, compassionate looks, and sentimental wishes for the future. The lump in my throat almost took my breath away. I still couldn't talk about my mother's loss without getting emotional. Hence, I tried not to get into long conversations with anyone. Josh came to the meeting last. We were waiting for him because he was the CEO's go-to person. Nothing in the publishing house took place without his knowledge.

The meeting went very smoothly. The next year's list of publications seemed quite impressive. The boss asked us for our opinion on several matters, noted down our suggestions, then thanked us for coming and invited us for coffee and cake in the conference room next door. I got up from my chair and rushed towards the exit, thirsty for another dose of caffeine.

'Could you stay for a minute, please,' asked Josh, who suddenly materialised beside me.

He waited for everyone else to leave the room and closed the door. I sat down at the table again. Seeing the serious face of my former lover, I was overwhelmed with anxiety and a premonition that something bad was in the air. He was still standing by the door as if to thwart my escape.

'Lucy,' he began in a soft but firm tone, 'I know you're going through a tough time right now, so I'm very sorry to add to your sack of problems ...'

I froze, cold shivers ran down my spine giving me goosebumps on my arms and neck. Droplets of sweat appeared on Josh's forehead seeing my reaction, he paused and then said:

'Unfortunately, in light of recent events, I am forced to end your employment with us.'

'What events?!' I coughed out, and uncontrollably my eyes filled with tears.

Josh sat down next to me in a chair. He leaned toward me and whispered:

'I shouldn't be telling you this because if the boss finds out, he will kick out both of us ... The official reason for your dismissal is the restructuring of the company.'

'I don't understand ...' I shook my head in total bewilderment.

'A few days ago, Martin paid a visit to my office and said that he had received an offer he could not refuse.'

'Who from?'

'He said he couldn't tell me that for now. He just said that our publishing house has the opportunity to sign some extremely favourable new contract.'

'That's probably a good thing, isn't it?'

He affirmed with a slight tilt of the head, with some embarrassment.

'The point is that one of the conditions for signing it is to reduce our staff ... by your person.'

'What the hell?' I blurted out with a tight throat. 'Why me?'

'I have no idea.'

'Are you actually joking me?!' I jumped up from my chair and began to walk around the room nervously. 'It must be some kind of joke!' I insisted.

'I'm afraid not,' he replied, disillusioning me. 'The best option for you will be dismissal by agreement of both parties. Go for it, then you will get a severance pay, the equivalent of three months' salary.'

I felt that I was losing the use of my limbs, so I slumped into the nearest chair. I sat for a moment in complete stillness, barely restraining myself from crying.

'I'm so sorry, Lucy ... Especially after everything we've been through together.'

The touch of Josh's fingers on my shoulder gave me an unpleasant shiver. I shook off his hand with a wave of my arm and pulled back.

'So, what you're saying is that I am getting kicked out cause some *hot shot arse wipe writer* waved a new contract in front of the CEO's nose ...? Despite all my hard work?! That's how you respect dedicated employees in this company?!' I hissed.

'Sorry,' he whispered and looked down, trying to avoid the eye contact.

'You can shove your *sorry* up your arse, mate!' I growled and headed for the exit.

'Lucy ...! You still have to sign ...'

'Send me everything by e-mail. End of!' I said, slamming the door behind me.

I stormed out of the building without a word. When I got outside, I breathed violently as if I had been underwater. I was proud of myself that I had been able to stop myself from crying so far. I never cried in front of strangers. Now, however, tears came to my eyes. I felt wronged and hurt. It turned out that more than three years of hard work on manuscripts, calling at night to squeeze the greatest potential out of them, meant nothing.

A waterfall of bitterness and grief poured out of me in the car. Only after a quarter of an hour was I able to stop sobbing over my fate. I thought it was some kind of fate. How would I manage without work? After all, work was the one only thing that kept me sane in recent months!

I pulled my phone out of my bag. I just wanted to talk to someone. Just like that—with wine, under a blanket, with a tonne of tissues wet from tears and snot. I don't think I've ever felt lonelier than when I reached the last name of a long list of contacts where I couldn't find a single person to complain to.

My college friends have long gone to the farthest corners of the world. I never had close relationships with the people I worked with, except maybe Josh, but he was the last person I wanted to talk to at that moment. I was guilty of my loneliness. I avoided leaving the house, I worked virtually non-stop, and new characters usually appeared in my life only on the pages of novels.

One day, they will engrave me in gold letters with an inscription on a granite tombstone: 'Here lies Lucinda Marie Blackbird, recluse and workaholic. She lived a short and boring life. May she rest in peace.' And so be it. The inscription will quickly be overgrown with moss, because there will be no one to visit my grave anyway.

Filled to the brim with bitterness, swearing endlessly I drove off towards my house. However, instead of heading home I decided to pay Becky a flying visit, hoping that she would be able to lift my spirit, even temporarily.

***

'I think some friendly winds blew in this God-forsaken part of the world lately,' she joked, hugging me warmly.

I snorted, amused by her statement.

'I've had no visitors so far this week, but yesterday Gods of travels brought Johnny to me and now you.

Coincidence?! I think not,' she chuckled, waving her finger in the air theatrically.

'Sweet Mother of Jesus, hallelujah!' I said jokily, but the news about Harris's visit surprised me a little. I sat down in a hard office chair. 'Was it a nice visit?'

'Well, he had a quick coffee, brought us some money, and left.'

I whistled in amazement at his gesture. 'Good old John, ay?!' I said, trying not to reveal the mockery in my voice.

'Yeah!' she agreed oblivious to my sarcastic comment. 'I actually thought you'd come together like you did last time. I was curious if you had already recovered a bit from all the news you've been exposed to recently ...'

She looked at me intently as if to find out how much I knew. *Did John tell her what had happened ...? Did they even talk about me?*

Not knowing what to answer, I spread my arms in a gesture that Becky could interpret freely.

'He didn't stay long ... He was in a bit of a rush.'

'Didn't he say why?' I asked with curiosity.

'Of course, he didn't!' Becky burst out laughing. 'Getting him to open up is nothing short of a miracle. I think he only knows how to write about feelings in his books ...'

'Yeah, you don't have to tell me that,' I admitted sadly and shrugged. Becky looked at me suspiciously, sitting on the desk as usual.

'Are you okay, birdy?' she asked with concern in her voice and put her arm around me. My eyes at once filled with tears. 'Lucy, my dear ... What's wrong?

'Oh, where do I start ...' My voice quickly turned to sobs. I leaned over, hiding my face in my hands.

'Is it a long story or are you just having a bad day today, sunshine?' she asked, stroking my back.

'As long as a python's tail, unfortunately,' I blurted out crying.

The woman stood by me for a few minutes, then patted me on the shoulder and left the office without a word. I used this moment to embrace myself a little. I wiped my snotty nose with my sleeve and began to inhale through my nose, then slowly let it out through my mouth. With this technique, I usually managed to tame the raging emotions.

Soon she re-entered the room with a plate and a cup in her hands.

'There you go,' she said, placing them on the desk in front of me.

'What's that?' I asked stupidly.

'Cocoa and honey toast.'

'Cocoa?! For me?' I felt like a kid.

'Well, yes. Recent studies have proven that it's almost impossible to stay sad after eating honey toast and drinking cocoa,' she said, quite adamant.

'Seriously?' I squinted amused, looking for signs of making fun of me on her.

'See? It works. You are already smiling, and you haven't even tasted these delicacies yet!' She winked at me, pointing encouragingly to the plate.

'Thank you,' I said warmly.

She was a good person. Only with my mother did I feel equally safe.

'There's nothing to be thankful for, birdy. I do what I can. Contrary to appearances, I am a poor comforter ... My bag of good advice in case of various life ills probably has a hole at the bottom ... Or I just got burned out,' she said honestly. 'But I make delish cocoa, huh?'

'Mmm, delish indeed,' I agreed. 'Talking about the difficulties of life doesn't seem to have any long-term impact,' I said resignedly.

'Unfortunately, you are right,' she agreed, watching me stuff my mouth with a sandwich. 'But remember, I'm always here for you. Unlike Johnny, I have no problem answering questions, even difficult ones.'

I looked at her gratefully. If her sister had the same peace and wisdom as her, it is no wonder Harris missed her so much.

'I have a lot of questions, but to be honest, I don't think I'm mentally ready to hear the answers ...' I confessed.

'I understand. But let me ask you one thing. What is the real reason for your visit today?'

I shrugged.

'I don't really know,' I replied honestly. 'I just didn't want to be all alone today, I guess. I know I have to pull myself together and rearrange my life ... But it's hard to get used to life without mum. In addition, today, I have found out that I've lost my job ... And work was the last thing I could hold onto.'

Rebecca gave a nod of understanding.

'They say life will test you before it will bless you,' she said cautiously. 'It's different with this re-arrangement, Lucy. New does not always bring solace. Sometimes it's enough to just rearrange the old ... Sweep dust from the floor, open windows, settle more comfortably among familiar surroundings ... I can only give you one piece of advice: do not plan change too much and too quickly. Face life at your own pace. The solution will definitely appear ... It always does.'

'I hope you're right.'

'I speak from experience.' Saying that, her face became sad, and her eyes glazed.

I felt a strong need to change the subject.

'Did John seem okay?'

'We didn't say much. He was very absent,' she re-marked with regret. 'He only said that he had been dealing with the case of the man from the briefcase for several days and after investigating all the details, he realised that his case will take some time and energy to sort out.

I shook my head in disbelief.

'I still find it hard to understand how you two can discuss all of this with such stoic calm,' I confessed, not revealing my disapproval. 'After all, we are talking about the fate of living people! I know that they treated their partners badly, and this is outrageous, BUT these men are someone's sons, brothers, friends ...'

'There's no "but" in this situation,' she interrupted me dryly. 'After each case was closed, everyone involved had to deal with difficult emotions. However, I can assure you, every remorse was compensated when each woman could take her kids and start to live without fear and violence. With time, we even stopped remembering these men's faces, we only saw their deeds, which prompted us to make such decisions.'

'I don't know whether to admire you or feel sorry for you all.'

'Well ...' She spread her arms as if to let me know that it would not keep her awake at night. 'We all carry a cross on our backs. We all had to cope ... each in our own way. Some escaped into the world of books, others practised yoga, and some got drunk with whiskey, listening to jazz and smoking cigars.'

'Do you like to read?'

'No, but I can sit in the heron pose for up to ten minutes on each leg,' she laughed. 'The happy medium of life doesn't exist, but everyone eventually finds something that helps them cope with the world around them. Do you have something like it?'

'Yeah, work! Especially working on editing novels,' I replied bitterly. 'That was my job before I got the sack.'

She patted my hand comfortingly and said warmly: 'You can handle it, I'm sure of it, it will all work itself out. Sorry, birdy, but I have to go back to my duties. I hope you'll check in with me in a while, and your python's tail will get chopped at least in half,' she said and winked jokingly.

'I hope so too.'

'Good, that said ... I'm not kicking you out, but get out of here!' She laughed again. 'Good luck in finding a new job. And I will see you soon, I hope?!'

We said goodbye with a warm hug, and then she escorted me to the exit.

'Don't worry about Johnny,' she added as I stood in the doorway. 'He's a resourceful guy, he'll manage whatever he needs to do. He can always find a way to solve problems.'

On the way home, I stopped at Lidl and stocked up on food and alcohol. Shortly after I got back home, I opened the first bottle of wine and I fell into a ball of despair and self-pity.

Thursday, 20 October

Six days have passed since that fateful day at the publishing house and my dismissal. At first, anger prevailed. Inviting me to a meeting to discuss publishing plans for the next year, only to be told that it was no longer my business, was extremely snide. After all, it could have been handled differently, in a less humiliating way. Soon anger turned to despair, despair begot helplessness. I didn't have the strength to look for a new job yet. My days were filled with bitterness and a sense of injustice.

For as long as I can remember, I have always tried to meet all expectations that were thrown at me, regardless of whether they appeared at work or from my loved ones. I was conscientious, organised, I devoted my free time and all my life energy to perform the task entrusted to me well. And what did it give me in the end? Nothing whatsoever.

I realised that all my life I had walked paths that led me nowhere. I stood at a crossroads to realise that I achieved nothing. A lonely orphan, an unemployed old spinster with no prospects for the future—that's who I was.

My mother's death shook the ground beneath my feet. I struggled to find the balance as such. Then I met Harris, who messed with my head with his stories that completely changed the image of what I had believed to be true all my life.

And now the job ...

Bitterness poured out of me at every opportunity like middle aged blokes' fat from the tight speedos on the beach in Hunstanton. I tried to drown it with hectolitres of wine, deluding myself that it would help me fall asleep. The nights, however, were the worst. The lack of work had a destructive effect on my head. I was not even allowed to finish the text entrusted to me earlier. It was officially demanded to be returned to another editor. It finally got me down, and it felt like a slap in the face.

The next morning did not herald changes in my hope-less mood. Restless rains ruffled the crowns of birch trees at the entrance to the property, and I waved a white flag in this war with life.

I sat on the bed and looked around the bedroom. It looked like something out of Metallica's *Whiskey in the Jar* music video. Scattered dirty clothes virtually covered the entire floor except for the narrow path from the bed to the bathroom. Plates and cups piled up on the furniture, looking at me with mouldy eyes. On the windowsill stood an even row of empty wine bottles. Soon there will be no space for new ones.

I hid under the covers and felt a rustling packaging under my foot. With a few angry movements, I kicked the empty crisp packets out of the bed. I didn't feel like getting out of bed at all, but after a few days at home, I finally had to get out and do some shopping. Nothing could have motivated me more than the lack of wine and an empty fridge. The return to civilisation required a quick shower and washing of hair. I even shaved my armpits and calves, which was an achievement itself in my current mindset. Unfortunately, I could not find any reasonably clean clothes to wear. I looked in the wardrobe, but apart from the summer dresses and ski suit, there were only a few lavender moth pendants hanging inside.

So, I put on a creamy, flowery summer dress and went to the kitchen to make myself a cup of coffee. I put the kettle on the burner of the gas stove, and then went to the living room, hoping to find a jumper or sweatshirt in this horrible mess of mine. I had a similar mess in my head. I couldn't find anything useful there either. Getting drunk and feeling sorry for myself lately became my core activity, all other chores like doing my washing, or cleaning, patiently awaited its turn on the backseat in my head. The chaotic search did not bring a find in the form of a more decent sweatshirt or jumper, so I put a short down jacket directly on top of the summer dress, beige wedge boots had to do as well.

'Come on, Lucy, it's time to pull yourself together, girl!' I whispered to the reflection in the mirror before leaving the house.

In the car park, I greeted my neighbour briefly, who grimaced about my undoubtedly stunning appearance. I left as quickly as possible and entered the shop.

Life in a small-town flow somehow slower than in the city. Residents out of pure boredom try to entertain themselves with basic attractions. They usually know more about the others than the others know about themselves. When you—God forbid—come across a friend in a shop or on the street, they will do their best to squeeze you of any information like a sponge. In addition, they will prove to be an expert in every field. I've long learnt that it's safer not to talk to anyone, or even smile amicably.

I began my shopping hastily, without making eye contact with anyone. I slipped through the first alley, avoiding

Angela—a hairdresser with forty years of experience in poking her nose into others' affairs. Satisfied with this clever dodge, I rushed towards the alcohol shelf. I leaned over to browse through the assortment of white wines. After a while, someone behind me laughed. I turned my head.

'Can I help you?' I asked dryly.

'Nice outfit,' said the woman with a sneer.

'Excuse me?!'

'I SAID A NICE OUTFIT!' she repeated much louder. 'Have you suffered from a hearing loss in recent years?'

'Not that I recall, I was just surprised by your comment. Now, excuse me, miss, I would like to continue my shopping if I may.'

'Miss?!' she laughed. 'Lucy, for flip's sake! Don't you recognise me?'

I had no idea who this woman was. If she hadn't said my name, I would have been sure she mistook me for someone else. I took a closer look at her, desperately trying to remember how I could know her. She was short, with wavy blonde hair flowing around her shoulders and slender neck, and a beautiful tan. Not excessively beautiful but well-groomed and smelt of expensive perfume.

'I'm most sorry but I don't,' I said with a slight embarrassment.

'It's me, silly, Ginny!' she announced, winking at me.

'Ginny Bikini, now I'll be dammed!' I said incredulously. 'Christ, you've changed so much, girl!'

I came closer and hugged her warmly.

'Well, what can I say? I get better with age, like a good wine. College wasn't my prime time, obviously, hah?' She laughed.

'You look great,' I complimented, and she accepted the compliment with a wave of her hand. 'Tell me how you are doing?'

'Gladly, but not here,' she replied and with a brief dip of her chin pointed at Angela, lurking around the corner. 'Maybe we could meet up a bit later for a girls' night in? What you reckon? We could reminisce about good old days in private. Here walls have ears ... I'll drop by your house later with some wine. I rarely visit the UK, I live in sunny Spain now. I've just completed selling my studio apartment my parents bought for me when I was at Uni. There is no point in keeping it, as I'm not planning to move back here any time soon. My parents moved to Germany a few years ago, so nothing keeps me here really. What about you? Do you still live on Russell Street?'

'Yep, same house ...' I confirmed cautiously because I haven't hosted anyone in a long time. On the other hand, drinking wine with a friend from school seemed slightly less morally reprehensible than drinking alone again.

A flashback of an image of my messy house ran a shiver down my spine. A potential visit will at least mobilise me for an express cleaning session. At the end of the day, I had nothing else to do.

'Five o'clock?' I blurted out, preventing myself from changing my mind. 'What kind of wine do you like?'

'Cheap and good, preferably semi-sweet,' she laughed.

'Great, then I'll sort out some snacks.'

'Ginny, how about calimocho like in the old days?' I offered, amused by the idea. I almost felt the sweet taste of cola mixed with wine in my mouth.

'That's a blast from the past! Sure, thing sugar tits!' she reacted enthusiastically. 'I'll get some crisps and maybe a trifle?'

'That sounds like a good idea.'

'More like a recipe for a diarrhoea, but hey ho, you only live once, don't you?!' My friend burst out laughing, and the nosy hairdresser took another step towards us. 'I'll see you later. Yeah?'

'Not if I see you first!'

Ginny walked away with a swift step. I walked her to the cash register and dived back into the lower shelves in search of cheap semi-sweet wine. Then I put two bottles in the basket and in the next aisle, I added two cokes. I couldn't stop smiling, thinking about our plans for the evening.

'You had an argument with that Mercedes guy, huh?' It sounded behind me as I put my bags in the boot.

'Pardon?!' I asked indignantly.

An elderly hairdresser tottered toward me, clasping two plastic bags in her unsteady hands as she shuffled along.

'He sat in the car in front of your house a couple of times, but he didn't get out. He smoked a cigar every time and then drove away. Hence my conclusion that you must have argued.'

'I don't know anything about it,' I replied, closing the boot.

'Not too old for you?' continued the woman. 'What would your mother say to that? God rest her soul.'

'You know what?! It's none of your bloody business. I also suggest going and talking to someone who actually gives a shit about what you have to say,' I replied, as I did not care what she thought of me. 'Goodbye.'

I got into the car, ignoring what else she had to say to me and hurried out of the car park. The woman's words, however, stuck with me alone all the way home. I parked in front of the house and was about to take my shopping out of the boot when it occurred to me that I should check for any signs of John's recent visits. I went out in front of the entrance gate, crossed the street and looked around. Right next to the curb lay three cigar butts soggy from the rain. I picked up one of them, which still showed a paper ring showing the brand. I didn't know anything about cigars, but the picture on the paper and the inscription looked identical to those smoked by Harris.

So it means the old hairdresser was right. He actually was here. But why?

That old sod was a walking enigma to me. The fact that he stubbornly avoided answering simple (at least from my point of view) questions, filled me to the brim with distrust, fear but also burning curiosity. For this last reason, I could not erase him from my memory and move on without explaining his riddle.

I smiled crookedly at the thought that, apparently, he too could not cut the ties and forget about me. A strange system of mutual dependence arose between us, which at first glance seemed very far-fetched. However, I was convinced that eventually our paths would cross again.

Entering the house, I noticed an overflowing mailbox. I emptied it and took all the correspondence to the kitchen. I threw a pile of envelopes and advertising leaflets into the basket by the breadbin. I didn't have time to, even briefly, go through them. I felt the pressure of Ginny's upcoming visit.

I quickly unpacked my shopping and started cleaning. I put the washing on, changed the sheets, got rid of the empty wine bottles, and packaging of questionably nutritious snacks I'd filled my stomach with over the past weeks.

After a few hours of hard work, I finally put the house in order and collapsed exhausted on the couch. I would have liked to take a nap, but my empty stomach would not let me forget it was there and in need of some food. I dragged myself off the couch. I knew that I had to eat something before Ginny's visit, otherwise I would get drunk too quickly AGAIN.

I cut a circle in a slice of bread with a glass and fried it in butter, plugging the hole with an egg. It was my favourite snack served by my mother on Sunday mornings.

A cup of tea to go with it and I could conquer the world. I smiled sadly at this pleasant memory of the wonderful times when my mother's presence seemed obvious and a given.

I fell back on the couch again, this time with a book. I quickly fell asleep. When I heard the vigorous knock on the door, I jumped from the couch, quite confused. I looked at my phone, it just turned four o'clock.

'All right, my lovely?'

'Hi, you're an hour bloody early, girl!' I said surprised by her presence.

'Nope, it's five past five, stupid.'

I stood there for a second, stunned by her confidence. And replied: 'Well, maybe in Spain it is, but here in England, it's only four!'

'Oh shit! You are right! Should I come back in an hour then?'

'Don't be daft. Come on in.'

Ginny rolled her eyes, then followed me into the kitchen, a place where we used to spend most of our time when she came to see me years ago. 'Bloody hell!' she said after a moment. 'Hardly anything has changed here since our college days! This place still has the same vibe, doesn't it?'

'Yeah, that's true,' I replied proudly.

'That would be enough for an introduction,' she laughed. 'Where do you keep your glasses because I forgot? I'm dying of thirst.'

'In the cupboard above the sink,' I said amused. Amazingly, she made me feel light and carefree.

I pulled Coke and wine out of the fridge, ice cubes from the freezer, and put it all on the table in the living room. Ginny followed me with glasses in her hand.

'Which one is *bartendering* today?'

'Bartending,' I corrected her reflexively and smiled as I saw her roll her eyes.

'Don't be a smart Alec ... pour.'

'I'm pouring, my lady.' I laughed seeing a thirst painted all over her lips.

We toasted the meet up and took a sip of the calimocho we used to drink when life seemed much simpler.

'Delish! I reckon that tomorrow we will be hanging!'

'It seems so.'

'I don't have to get up for work,' she said amused.

'Neither do I, so cheers!' I picked up my glass.

'Are you off work tomorrow?'

'No, I'm unemployed.'

'Oh, shit, sorry, mate, I didn't know. Do you need any money?' she asked with concern.

'You're a plonker!' I laughed again. 'I'm okay, fear not. I got a severance pay, financially I am fine ... But the lack of work gets to me. A job has always been the cure for all my ills. And now I have nothing to do ...' I confessed, and the smile turned into a pitiful grimace. 'Eh, I have to admit, I've been falling apart lately.'

'A workaholic's worst nightmare, ay?'

'Something like that. First, my mother's illness knocked me down, then her death literally swept me off my feet. Immediately afterwards, Harris stepped in and disturbed the whole picture in my head, and now they fired me from work ... I'm telling you, one thing after another ...'

'So we don't like Harris then? Who is he anyway?!' she asked and frowned her eyebrows.

'Well, we do, and we don't ... Let's just say that for now, I have more important things to sort out in my head than John.'

'Who?'

'Harris, John Harris, my mum's old friend,' I explained with a gentle smile.

'Oh, like Bond, James Bond?' she replied, laughing, and held her hands out like a gun straight at me.

'You crack me up!' I laughed.

'Talking about crackers ... I'm very sorry for your loss. Your mum was a firecracker. Sometimes my mother and I remember her in our conversations,' she said sadly. 'I can only imagine how you are feeling right now ... When it comes to this guy who messed up your life, kick him in the arse and cut yourself off completely, that's the best way. Plus, I'm sure you will find a job soon, after all, you are a smart girl.'

I snorted indulgently because I knew it wasn't as easy as it seemed.

'To be honest, I don't want to talk about it all, not today,' I admitted sadly. 'You better tell me how you're doing.'

Ginny sighed.

'Well ... After graduating from college, I went to Uni but didn't like it there too much, so I took a year out, I went to Spain and find some work on an olive farm. And somehow it turned out that I stayed. Life is easier there than here. The weather is a dream. Maybe life is even easier in bigger cities, but I prefer to live in the countryside. I'm a peasant of flesh and blood.'

'You're right,' I said, making another drink. 'A lot of people left and never came back. All in all, it is not surprising. If it wasn't for the fact that I couldn't leave my mother, I probably would have been blown away somewhere. Still picking olives?'

'Nope. Now I have a full-time job in an old people's home. It's hard work, but I like to spend time with the oldies. Most of them are still quite switched on and you can talk to them on many interesting topics. You know, they used to be as young as us, they had their families, their careers, and they had adventures and romances. Many people forget about it and treat old people like some freaks. It's so sad when you think about it ...'

'Very sad. I admire your empathy, and so do they, I bet.'

'There's nothing to admire, mate.'

'I think there is. Since you devote time and attention to them. It certainly means a lot to them.'

'Most of them are lonely, so time is the worst enemy at times. I like to make it more pleasant for them, and that's it,' she said modestly and raised a toast to the meet-up again. Then she moved from the armchair to the couch, facing me. 'Okay, Lucy-Lue, now let's get down to business. Are you seeing someone then? Some guy or girl, no judgment ...? Is that Harris you mentioned your ex?'

'Harris?!' I laughed, shaking my head to let my friend know she couldn't have been more wrong if she tried. 'None of that. He's the guy I was supposed to help finish the novel. That was one of my mother's last wishes ... They used to be friends, back in the day. But it didn't work out.'

'Ah, right. Well, if it didn't work out, it didn't work out. You can't help it. Well, but I guess you have someone?'

I shook my head.

'I guess I'm cursed ... Or simply my relationships are doomed to failure.'

'You talk crap,' she protested. 'Love is not a matter of luck but a set of coincidences.'

'Coincidences?'

'Well, yes. Hear me out: we are always getting to know people, every day, you might even say. But we only feel a spark with certain people, right?'

It was hard to disagree.

'If we want that spark, we need to be at the right place and at the right time come across this special person, and on top of that, we have to be equally open to the possibility of it all. Let's not even mention the visual qualities and disposition. So many things have to happen at once for us to get struck by Cupid's arrow. Isn't that right?'

'Well, yes,' I agreed with her.

'All it takes to miss it all is to leave the house a moment later, change our mind about going somewhere or simply pass this someone special. And that's it. Our chance for love flies away.'

'There is a method to this madness,' I admitted and raised my glass. 'Cheers.'

'To coincidences! *Salud!*'

'*Salud!*'

'And a loo.'

'And cheers to the loo?!' I asked surprised.

'No, stupid. I need a wee.'

'Ah! First door on the right.'

'I remember!' she finished the rest of the calimocho and handed me an empty glass. 'Pour, I'm going to make room in my bladder. Could you bring something to eat in the meantime? I left the shopping bag on the kitchen counter ...'

I saluted to her request like a soldier and jumped off the couch.

'Your wish is my command, my lady! I'll grab it. You go toilet, otherwise you're going to have to ask me where I keep the mop,' I grumbled. Alcohol was pleasantly buzz-ing in my head.

Just when I was putting snacks on the plate, my eyes fell on the pile of letters that I had pulled out of the mail-box earlier. I flipped through them briefly. My attention was caught by a grey envelope. I frowned seeing familiar handwriting.

I ripped the envelope open impatiently.

Becky said you were looking for a job. This offer fell into my hands by accident. You have the details on the leaflet. I realise that this is a completely different kind of work from the one you have been doing recently, but they pay very well, the position seems interesting, and it's not too much of a drive. You will do as you see fit. I think it's worth a try. Take care—J.

I set the letter aside and read the attached booklet briefly.

'What's that?' asked Ginny, looking over my shoulder.

'A job offer.'

'Show me!' She unceremoniously took the leaflet out of my hand and began to read aloud, 'Moore Supplies company dealing with the distribution of office products. Position of assistant to a member of the Management Board. Work in the office from Monday to Friday, from nine to five, plus business trips. Salary: twenty-nine grand per annum ... That's not bad, is it?'

'Not bad at all,' I admitted.

'And they also offer a Christmas bonus ... So much for the flyer. Why don't we take a look at their website?'

Obediently, I reached for my mobile phone on the table next to the couch and typed in the address of the website.

'Give it, I'll read, and you have a think if it's cool,' Ginny announced, taking over the phone. 'Blah, blah, blah ... We already know that. Oh, there is a job description. Listen: replying to customer emails, preparing SEO texts, perfecting content using AI, completing company documentation, participating in board meetings and preparing relevant documents, cooperation with sales and marketing departments, direct cooperation with board members, participation in conferences and business meetings according to the company's needs ... Can you grasp such things?'

'I guess I could handle it ... Anyway, I'm a fast learner.'

'Coolio Julio!' she said, not taking her eyes off the screen. 'Wait, I have to finish reading because I'm already starting to mix the letters ... Our requirements: communicativeness, willingness for development and positive attitude. You have?'

'I have,' I laughed.

'French at a communicative level ... Hm, do you speak French?

'*Oui je le fais!*' I said enthusiastically.

'What?' She looked at me with an unintelligent face. 'Okay, I'll take your word for it ... I'm reading further: we require very good organisation skills. The ability to work with text and SEO tools is welcome but not mandatory. We supply comprehensive training.' Ginny raised her eyebrows in approval. 'And finally: we offer work in an independent position, attractive remuneration, industry training, a relaxed non-corporate atmosphere, freedom of action, work in the industry of the future, which is not afraid of recession, as well as direct cooperation with industry experts.'

I had to admit that the offer was really interesting. As a matter of fact, I have never worked as an assistant before, but I was interested in the elements of working on the texts—this is what I specialised in. In addition, the possibility of business trips and training appealed to me.

'And? What you reckon?' asked Ginny sipping another drink. 'Do you think this is an offer for you?'

'I'm not sure ... But if I don't try, I will never know I guess.'

'Right, call them!'

'Right now?!'

'Yeah! You know what they say ... you snooze, you lose.'

I thought it might have already happened. I didn't know how long John's letter had been in my mailbox.

'It might be a bit too late to call them today.' Suddenly, I had doubts.

'Well, it might be nearly six o'clock in Spain, but it's not even five here,' she said and winked at me. 'In the leaflet, it says that they work until five.'

'But I'm already half-cut!'

'Good, that can only help! Call them, I said.'

I dialled the number with a sense of hopefulness. As we talked, an enthused woman on the other end of the line exclaimed that the position was still available! I thought, 'Is this for real?' With a massive dose of courage, I asked if she liked working there. Even though my interviewee likely was a marketer, her enthusiasm about working at Moore Supplies was infectious. Under Ginny's watchful eye, I figured why not? And so, I updated my CV, filled out the application form and sent my required documentation to the e-mail address provided in the colourful brochure. After all, maybe this could be the start of something pretty darn exciting. 'You can type like lightning,' said Ginny, watching me with admiration.

'Practice makes perfect,' I replied modestly, closing my laptop. 'Okay, we have something to drink for. Thanks for pushing me to do all this, my darling, you are a Godsend.'

'No *problemo!*' She smiled meaningfully, devouring mini pork pies with crisps and peanuts.

'Let's just hope they will like what they see on my CV and put my name down for an interview,' I said cautiously.

'Why wouldn't they take you on?! You are smart, young, and good with words! I'm telling you; I feel like this is a new beginning for you,' she declared with conviction. 'I'll make it happen for you!'

That said, she began to rub her hands vigorously against each other, then touched the leaflet with one hand and my forehead with the other.

'What are you doing?' I laughed.

'I'm giving you positive energy from the Universe, you fool! What does it look like?!'

'You crazy witch!' I said fondly.

'Not a word ...' She shrugged. 'There are no jokes when it comes to the power of cosmic awesomeness. One false move, and the waves will accumulate badly and instead of a new job you will get diarrhoea ...'

'Okay, you do your thing. Shitting myself now is the last thing I want.'

We polished off the last of the wine but were far from finished with our evening. Like a pair of schoolgirls, we called a taxi and made our way to the nearest petrol station. They should have known better than to sell us half a litre of tequila, given the devilish grins painted on our faces.

We tumbled back into the house, giggling about how perfect this day was—we were finally doing something for ourselves. We crashed on the couch in a heap of empty bottles and glassy-eyed laughter, both knowing this was exactly what we needed to feel alive.

Tuesday, 25 October

'Hi, my name is Lucy Blackbird. I'm scheduled for an interview at twelve-thirty,' I said to the woman behind the desk. She tore her eyes away from the monitor, measuring me with a disapproving look from the red-rimmed glasses slid down to the tip of her nose.

'What's your name?!' she asked as if she hadn't heard the first time. She had a nasty look on her face, and her voice was clearly haughty.

'Like I said, my name is Lucy Blackbird.'

'Third floor,' she said with exaggerated mouth. 'After exiting the lift, the third door on the left.'

'Thank you,' I said dryly.

I stared at my reflection in the elevator's mirror, adjusting the black dress that hugged my body perfectly. My shoes produced a staccato sound as I boldly headed towards the room as directed by the receptionist. I pushed open the glass doors and surveyed the space in front of me. A small waiting room with two chairs and office posters plastered on the walls. No doubt marketing was not this company's forte; not one but two syntax errors were splashed across their promotional slogans. I went to one of the posters and started reading the small text at the bottom of it.

'No comma, spelling mistake at the end of the second line, and typo, dear God,' I whispered, shaking my head in disbelief.

'Where's the mistake?' Suddenly, a man's voice sounded behind me.

'Oh, here.' I touched just below the sign with my finger and turned my head towards the man. He approached and stood next to me. He pulled a red sharpie from his pocket and marked the place of the error on the glass with a circle.

'Typo here,' he continued. 'And where is it missing the comma?'

'After the word "times," here.'

'All right, thank you,' he said brusquely and entered the office without closing the door behind him. I poked my head round to look inside. The man sat down in a leather chair behind an elegant desk, pressed a button on his phone on the desktop, and articulated in a firm tone:

'Emma, please send Charlie over to my office.'

'Sure, boss, right away,' replied the woman in a shrill voice.

'Please, come in,' he called me with an inviting gesture of his hand. 'How can I help you?'

'I came for a job interview.'

'I see,' he replied politely. 'And for what position?'

Thus speaking, he got up from behind his desk and walked over to the small table by the window. He pushed back his chair and asked me to sit down.

'Assistant to a board member,' I replied, nodding slightly in thanks, and extended my hand in greeting. 'My name is Lucy Blackbird.'

'Michael Moore, nice to meet you, Lucy.' The man shook my hand lightly, then waited patiently for me to hang my coat over the armrest of the chair and sit comfortably. 'Let me guess: the receptionist directed you to the third door on the left. Am I wrong?'

'No, that's right,' I said, slightly confused.

'She probably meant the other "left".' He laughed.

'Oh no, I'm so sorry!' I said, blushing. Indeed, in this affair, I confused the directions! 'Please excuse me for the intrusion.'

'It's okay,' he said hastily, seeing me jump up from my chair. 'Please stay a little longer.'

The next second, a breathless man in a grey shirt, black suit trousers, and bright trainers appeared in the doorway.

'Boss wanted to see me?' he gasped.

'Yes,' Moore admitted, closing his hands on his stomach. 'You know how much I care about the professional image of my company, don't you?'

'Of course!' assured the newcomer zealously.

'At all levels!' specified the boss. 'Am I right in thinking that you have been responsible for the graphic side of things since Marbel retired?'

'Yes, boss,' the man replied, completely confused.

Moore looked at me questioningly.

'There are some mistakes on one of the posters on the wall, there,' I said quietly and pointed on the wall in next room. I dared not look at the man standing near me, not wanting to embarrass him even more.

'Exactly. Such mistakes significantly reduce the value of the company's promotional materials. I suggest paying more attention to your work. Please remove the C17 posters from the walls, correct the errors and have them printed again. Thank you.'

'Yes, boss, I'm sorry,' the employee stammered and hurriedly left. He went up to the wall in the waiting room, pulled off the written frame and left, threw a bunch of obscene words under his breath—a little too loud for the boss not to hear, then walked out, quietly closing the door behind him.

'I feel terrible,' I confessed. 'I shouldn't have said anything. I just caused that man trouble.'

'On the contrary,' he assured me. 'Don't worry. What time was your interview?'

'Twelve-thirty,' I said and grimaced, checking the time on my watch, which I always wore on my wrist.

'Well, you're late,' Moore commented. 'Come with me then.'

I shrugged off my coat and strode confidently after him down the glowing hallway. He gave a curt nod and held open the door for me like I was royalty or something. I offered him a sardonic smirk in return. We stepped into a cavernous conference room—only two figures seated around the gigantic, curved table; a rotund old lady, her face creased with age, and a wiry man with shocking-white hair. Conversation abruptly ceased as they caught sight of us—still with smiles plastered on their faces though.

'Good morning,' said the boss from the entrance, gesturing them not to bother with getting up and unnecessary pleasantries. 'Here's your "twelve-thirty",' he introduced me, rather non-standard. 'Could I take a look at her CV, please?'

'Of course,' replied the woman, handing him the document from the briefcase in front of her.

'Please sit down,' said the skinny man kindly, pointing to the chair on the opposite side of the table.

'I'm so sorry for being late, I got lost,' I excused myself.

'No worries,' said the boss carelessly as if I were directing those words to him and not to the couple sitting across from me.

Moore read my CV with concentration, with his eyebrows drawn. My heart was thrashed wildly. After a few minutes of tormenting silence, he said:

'For Tom?'

'Yes, boss,' replied the skinny man.

'All right. Is she the last one?' he asked enigmatically.

'One before last,' replied the woman, equally cryptically.

'In that case, come and see me after the last one. Thank you.' That said, he put the document on the table, then turned towards me, sent a friendly smile, and left.

The couple at the table looked at each other meaningfully. The woman closed the briefcase and secured its contents with an elastic band.

'Thank you, Miss Blackbird. That's all for today,' she said.

The skinny man must have guessed my confusion, for he got up and walked over to the door, which he opened invitingly in front of me. I rose obediently from my seat, still in shock.

'I bet you've never been to such a quick interview, have you?' the woman asked. This time her voice seemed strangely familiar to me.

'Never,' I admitted, still not knowing what to think about it all.

'You spoke to me on the phone last week,' she said, friendly.

'Oh, that's why your voice seemed familiar to me.' I smiled.

'And just out of curiosity ... What impression did Mr Moore make on you?'

'Pardon?' I asked surprised by her question.

'I mean, did he intimidate or scare you ...'

'He rather impressed me,' I said swiftly.

'In that case, thank you, we will get back to you soon!'

'Uh ... Thank you!'

I walked out, carefully closing the door behind me. While I was waiting for the lift, the company graphic designer I had met earlier and put in a rather uncomfortable situation passed me in the hallway.

'Sorry, Charlie, isn't it?!' I blurted out without thinking.

'Yeah?' He stopped a few steps away from me.

'I am deeply sorry for pointing out your mistakes earlier ... I didn't want to cause you any trouble,' I said, smiling apologetically. 'The thing is that I have been proofreading texts for so many years that I'm doing it without thinking.'

'No worries, this isn't the first and certainly not the last time I got told off,' he reassured me. 'I'm good at graphics. Words are not my strong point ... But you already know that!' He laughed hoarsely. 'I have to skedaddle to cock something else up! There is no time to lose! Ta ta.'

I didn't know how to interpret this man's behaviour. Did he mock me or himself? I haven't been so confused in a long time.

***

My fingers hovered over the car door handle, but I paused when my nostrils prickled with the aroma of something utterly delicious. I spun around, searching for the source of this heavenly goodness. My empty stomach growled loudly, reminding me that I had skipped breakfast in a state of jittery pre-interview nerves.

My gaze landed on a little greasy spoon nearby and my mouth salivated at the thought of a home-cooked meal. Without hesitation, I strolled up to it, thinking that the interior wouldn't make a good impression on me. But upon entering, I was pleasantly surprised—gone were the tacky decor and tatty furniture, replaced by modern interiors and a wall decorated with colourful paintings. The glass counter proudly displayed hot dishes; it was like being in a cozy, homely pub.

This wasn't the low-budget eatery I remembered from my university days! Here, even the chairs and tables were painted white and green. With its friendly service and aesthetically appealing design, it felt more like a chic dine-in restaurant than any greasy spoon I had ever seen.

The restaurant was a haven. As soon as I stepped through the door, I knew that I'd be staying there for longer than anticipated. The air was full of tantalising aromas and the chatter of people exchanging pleasantries with the staff.

I ordered a full English breakfast and an ice-cold Coke, then found my seat at the only remaining table in the corner—right near an outlet! I pulled out my phone and fired up Audible to find a new audiobook for the journey home.

'May I?' asked a man with a bacon sandwich and a plate of chips in his hands.

He had a low, raspy voice that for some reason sent shivers down my spine.

'Sure,' I said, lingering my eyes on his cheerful face. I smiled back and pointed with my hand to the empty chair opposite.

'Cheers, it's a bit crowdy here today.'

'The food is delicious and cheap, I reckon, so that's probably why,' I said.

'That's correct and above all, it's on the high street. Do you eat here often? I don't think I've ever seen you here before,' he asked, scoffing the sandwich.

'I'm here for the first time,' I replied while the waiter put a plate with my order on the table in front of me. 'Enjoy your meal,' he said and left.

'Thank you,' I replied and shifted my gaze to the display of my phone, searching for the next book to listen to.

'Hmmm ...' muttered my companion.

I looked at him questioningly.

'I wanted to chat you up, but I can't think of any brilliant lines,' the man said with disarming sincerity.

He made me laugh, saying that.

'I find it hard to believe that someone like you has a problem with talking to women,' I laughed.

'Someone like me? Means what? Handsome, intelligent, and charming?' he retorted, dragging his hand over his curly hair.

'Don't forget to add humble,' I said cheerfully and winked jokingly.

'You winked at me!' he was pleased. 'So, I'm doing great?'

'Doing great what?!'

'Casting my spell on you, silly! So, am I? Is it working?'

'Like a charm,' I said, giggling.

'You have a beautiful smile,' he said, impaling the last chips on his fork.

'Thank you, I inherited my mother's smile. Same as teeth, and they fit perfectly!' I added seriously.

The guy looked at me surprised, and when he understood my crude joke, he choked with laughter.

'Oh my!' he said, still shaking his head.

'Well, you see, not only handsome and charming intellectuals have a problem with pickup lines. Slim brunettes of medium height as well.'

'Lord, have mercy on us, there is no salvation for us!' he said, then raised his glass with what was left of his drink.

'Amen!' I joined the toast.

'It's probably the nicest lunch I've had this year,' he said.

'I'm very pleased to hear that. I haven't laughed like that for a long time either. Thank you.'

'The pleasure is all mine.'

'On the contrary, I insist that it is mine as well.'

'We should not be arguing on the first date.'

'Date? Damn, if I'd known I'd be dating at a greasy spoon today, I would have definitely tried to impress you more.'

'I think you're doing great. I wouldn't change a thing. Nothing at all.'

'Your words lift a weight from my heart, igniting joy that sparks through my soul like a living flame,' I replied with exaggerated drama, pressing the back of my hand to my forehead.

'And the thought of our time together will paint roses on our cheeks forever after parting?' he added amused.

'Surely, O noble sir.'

'O lady, before the direction of our paths separates us forever, tell me your name!'

'What's in a name? That which we call a rose, by any other word would smell as sweet,' I recited, not expecting that the words of Shakespeare's balcony scene would be familiar to him.

'I know not how to tell thee who I am. My name, dear saint, is hateful to myself, because it is an enemy to thee. Had I it written, I would tear the word,' he continued the script, took my hand and pulled it gently toward his mouth*.

---

* William Shakespeare, *Romeo and Juliet* Act 2, scene 2 Second Quarto of 1599.

The romantic scene was interrupted by the signal of an incoming call. The man pulled the phone out of his pocket and, without letting go of my hand, answered the call.

'Hello? All right, give me two minutes,' he said and hung up. He hurriedly kissed my hand and got up from the table. 'I'm very sorry, but I have to get back to work. You don't even know how much I needed a moment like that ...'

'The pleasure is all mine, sir,' I replied. 'I say goodbye forever.'

'Or maybe just say: "see you again"?' he asked with a smile.

'Perhaps. See you then!'

As he strode out of the pub, a smug grin spread across his face while his hands nestled contentedly in his pockets. I let out an amused giggle that echoed off the walls, briefly catching the eye of the waitress, who seemed to share my amusement. Blushing, I quickly looked away, not wanting to be seen as too indulgent. His scent lingered behind him like a ghostly reminder of his presence, but he was gone, and all that remained was an empty chair before me.

'Could I ask for a piece of cheesecake to go?' I asked the guy by the checkout, not taking my eyes off the counter.

'Of course,' he replied and walked away toward the cake cabinet. I touched my cheek with my hand, checking to see if my face burnt as intensely as the thoughts in my head.

It was burning.

'You must have had a good time, hearing our conversation,' I said to the cashier as he placed the cardboard box of cake in front of me.

'It's a small place,' he replied without embarrassment. 'It's hard not to hear things ... And that was something!'

I thanked him and left. I got in the car and laughed, hiding my face in my hands. My cheeks were still burning.

'Oh, Lucy! You are such a twat sometimes,' I said self-critically, shaking my head.

I clicked on the first audiobook that grabbed my attention and headed home. Throughout the evening, a maelstrom of emotions battered my mind: disbelief, hope, joy, uncertainty. My thoughts were consumed by the extraordinary events of a brief visit to the city. A job interview like no other, followed by a simple lunch at a little café, where I could indulge in some people-watching. And then, there was him—a mysterious stranger with quick wit and flirty words, who stirred within me the desire for romance and adventure.

With every passing moment, I felt as though I was standing at the edge of a new chapter in my life. One filled with twists and turns that would both challenge and fulfil me. Finally, I was ready to take the plunge and sign my name on this next page.

Thursday, 27 October

'Good morning, Lucy. My name is Fiona Green, and I am calling from Moore Supplies.' A nice familiar voice came from the other end of the phone. 'Is this Lucy Blackbird, please?'

'Yes, good morning,' I said, holding my breath.

'I'm calling to officially offer you the position of an Assistant Board Member you applied for. Are you still interested in working for our company?'

'Of course!' I confirmed at once.

'In that case, congratulations and welcome aboard!'

'This is wonderful news, thank you very much.'

'You're welcome. I will send you the contract by e-mail, please read it and accept the terms in the return message.'

'Of course, thank you.'

'That's not a bother,' assured Fiona, cheerful notes echoing in her voice. 'Tell me please, when could you start? During our last conversation, we didn't have the opportunity to ask too many questions ...'

'That's true, it was quite a non-standard interview ...' I admitted. 'Monday?'

'Welcome to Moore Supplies, nothing is ordinary and standard here.'

'At least it's not boring.'

'That's it, we do not know what boredom is!' she laughed. 'If you have any questions, please call the number I'll attach to my email, and I'll see you on Monday at nine. Please report at the reception, they will direct you to the HR department.'

'Thank you and see you Monday then.'

'Goodbye.'

After what felt like an eternity of waiting, the e-mail finally popped up in my inbox. After glancing over the content of the contract, I had to pinch myself as everything was as favourable as it had been promised. Without a second thought, and with a heart full of anticipation, I confirmed the commencement date.

I wanted to express my delight at this new challenge, so I sent my lovely friend Ginny a message on Messenger—she was overjoyed for me and excitedly showed her enthusiasm with dozens of emojis and some hilarious gifs! My thoughts naturally turned to John who had informed me about the job vacancy at Moore Supplies, but I pushed the thought away. No matter how many flaws others saw in me, one thing they couldn't deny was my drive and determination.

Feeling that familiar need for yet more congratulations, I dialled Becky's number, but it went straight to her voicemail. Disappointed not to get to share my good news with her directly, I left her a short but sweet message informing her of my success.

I raised my mug of steaming Yorkshire tea in a silent salute to the photo of my mother, standing proudly on the table next to her favourite bookcase. I felt the familiar pang of longing and regret that came with missing her. I'd wanted so badly to feel her comforting embrace and inhale the scent of home once more.

But for now, I had a new chapter to focus on; one full of possibilities. I smiled to myself, feeling sure that if mum were here, she'd be proud of me for finding the strength to leave behind the dreary mediocrity of my past life. Yes, things were about to change—both inside and out—and I was ready.

Monday, 31 October

'Human Resources: fifth floor, room number thirteen.' *Phew, good job that I'm not superstitious,* I thought, reading the information on the wall in the lobby of the office building. I imagined the face the rude receptionist would make when she saw me, but for the moment, the reception desk was empty.

I took the lift upstairs and hurried to the indicated office. It took me less than a quarter of an hour to fill out the necessary forms. The woman working in the HR department turned out to be a rude, flat-arsed Karen— probably from sitting behind a desk for so many years. She took a picture of me and after a while handed me the badge on a lanyard in the company colours. Then she sent me to the seventh floor, wishing me a nice first day of work with a sarcastic smile painted all over her face.

I hung the badge around my neck and obediently headed for the elevator. The prospect of meeting a new boss made me both excited and stressed.

'Oh, I see that the interview was a success!' said the graphic designer from inside the lift. He moved, revealing the button panel, and I pressed the one with the seven. Then he put the box under his left arm and stretched out his right hand towards me. 'I'm Charlie. I don't think I had a chance to introduce myself properly last time.'

'Lucy,' I said relieved. I was glad that he did not take offense for the fact that I got him in trouble a few days earlier. I shook his hand tightly, in a masculine way. 'I'm sorry again for the other day ... Correcting mistakes has become my curse ...'

'No bother! At least from now on, I will know who to send projects to for the final approval before printing. As compensation for the harm you applied on me, of course,' he said and winked.

'No problem, there must be repentance,' I agreed. 'I will repent!'

'Who will you be working with?'

'Good question! I completely forgot to ask!'

'Then show me what it says on the back of your badge,' he said, bringing my ID closer to his eyes.

'Look, here you have your office number. It's a big office building, and it's easy to get lost here at the beginning. F7R10, see?' He pointed to the inscription with his finger. 'Seventh floor, room number ten. This means that you will work with Thomas Johnson, he's alright, you know.'

'Phew! Thanks.'

'Cool beans, I'm going to my office F7R25. From the lift to the left, you have odd numbers. So, your office is to the right!' he blared out at the speed of a machine gun and left me, even more confused.

After a few minutes, however, I managed to get to the right place. I took a deep breath and knocked gently on the door marked with the number ten plate. No one spoke, so I knocked louder.

'It is not a confessional, so that you have to knock. Enter!' I heard a man's voice.

In fact, I shouldn't have knocked. It was the nerves.

I opened the door and went inside. The small room with white walls resembled the one I had found myself in by mistake a few days earlier. I was separated from the boss's office by a partition wall painted in a dark blue colour. I went in further.

'Good morning,' I started politely but stopped when I recognised the man standing by the printer.

'Juliet?! You are shitting me!' exclaimed the guy from the greasy spoon. 'What the hell? Hi!'

'Hello,' I stammered, desperately trying to control the trembling of my voice and limbs. 'And what you doing here? Do you also work for Thomas Johnson?'

'No,' he laughed. 'I am Thomas Johnson. And you? Have you got lost?'

'Not at all,' I said. I came closer and showed him my ID.

'Holy shit, what a surprise!'

'Indeed,' I remarked, officially shaking his hand in greeting. 'My name is Lucy Blackbird.'

'I'm very pleased to meet you. Thomas Johnson or Tom, if you will,' he replied, taking my hand.

A wedding ring flashed on his finger, setting off alarm bells in my head.

'I hope that what I'm about to say won't be misunderstood by you, after all, you're my boss,' I said, trying to sound professional. 'However, I would like to ask that our relationship remain purely professional.' My eyes involuntarily went to the gold disc on his finger. 'Our innocent flirtation ended the moment we left the eatery. Agreed?'

'Of course!' he confirmed, nodding vigorously. 'Boss and assistant, purely professional relationship.'

'Excellent. Is this my desk?' I pointed to a piece of furniture under the window in a bright room behind the partition wall.

'Yes, make yourself comfortable,' he said, handing me a black-bound notebook. 'I've written down all the passwords and the general outline of your duties. Please familiarise yourself with them, and after lunch, I will explain all the other tasks to you and present your travel plan for the next three months.'

Tom left me alone, and I praised the architect, grateful that there was a partition wall that gave me a bit of privacy. My heart was pounding in my chest like Big Ben.

I hung my coat on a wall-mounted hanger, then sat down at my desk. My side of the office was equipped as standard: a computer, monitor, mouse on the company's pad, printer, photocopier, document shredder. In the drawer, I found pens, pencils, a stapler, and other office supplies.

I opened the black notebook with the company's logo that Tom handed me earlier. I read his notes, involuntarily noting the absence or excess of commas.

'Coffee or tea?' he sounded from behind the wall after a few minutes.

'Yes, please,' I replied.

'Okay, but which one: coffee or tea?' he laughed.

'Coffee! Although I think I should offer to make one for you ...'

'Today you can enjoy the privilege of a new starter,' he said, materialising before me. 'Come on, I'll show you the kitchen. We have a coffee machine, fridge, and microwave in there.'

It turned out that I would not have to go far to grab a coffee, the kitchen was in the next room. I decoded the instructions for using the coffee machine. Tom made me a latte and an Americano for himself.

'I want you to feel at ease here. Here and with me,' he clarified when we were back in our room. He waited for me to settle down behind my desk, then he pulled a chair for himself and sat down across from me. 'Neither of us could have predicted that we would become work colleagues.'

'That's true,' I admitted. I should have stopped there, but something tempted me to continue. 'Do you often eat lunches there and dazzle the women you meet with your knowledge of Shakespeare?'

'I eat there almost every day. In the company kitchen, I only use a kettle and a coffee machine. As for throwing Shakespearean rhymes ...' He smiled as if embarrassed. 'To be honest, I don't know what came over me that day.'

'So, was it an isolated case?' I asked dryly, remembering that he certainly didn't have a wedding ring on his finger that day. 'I wonder what your wife would say about that.'

Tom looked at me carefully. Maybe he was wondering what to say.

'My wife left me some time ago,' he said after a moment. 'She had stopped wearing her wedding ring long before I did. Taking it off will mean a symbolic breaking of the ties between us. And we don't have a divorce yet.'

'I see,' I said, wondering if he was being honest with me. 'Do you hope she'll come back?'

He shook his head in the negative.

'Not anymore. There is too much baggage between us ... We have become strangers to each other. I don't think there's anything left to fix,' he replied, and I believed him. I even felt a bit sorry for him. 'How about you? Any diamond ring on the horizon?'

'Nope, not that I know of,' I replied.

'But there must be someone special, somewhere close, I bet?' he became interested.

'Some time ago, I got involved in a relationship with no future. But it's over, so there's nothing to talk about either.'

'I'm sorry.'

I shrugged.

'No need. That relationship was doomed from the beginning.'

'A good life lesson, I presume?'

'Yeah, that's how I started to look at it.'

'Family?'

'My mother died of cancer less than four months ago. The rest of the family is also on the other side.'

'Accept my condolences.'

I nodded in thanks.

'How about you?' I asked, curiously. 'Do you have someone close to you?'

'No kids.' He looked at me meaningfully as if he thought that was what interested me the most. 'My mother has lived with her second husband in Denmark for over twenty years. We used to have a closer relationship, but over time, the contact has loosened a bit. I see my father more often, he lives not too far from me. I check in whenever I'm close by.'

'It's nice you have at least part of your family living nearby, I guess.'

Tom finished his coffee and stood up, leaving the empty cup on my desk.

'Enough talking for now, don't you think?' he asked with a distinct hint of irony in his voice. 'Off to work we go, Miss Blackbird.'

'Yes, sir!'

Called to order, I turned on the computer to check the e-mail box and view current messages on the company's server, according to Tom's suggestions.

After lunch, which I spent in the canteen, getting to know other co-workers, Johnson and I discussed the most urgent tasks. The day flew by in a flash. Email from HR informed me that my next working day will be my induction—I hated it nearly as much as manual handling and health and safety training. A short conference call about a new line of office equipment sold by the company to the French market was planned an hour before workday ended. I said goodbye to my boss and informed him about my schedule for the next day.

Tom seemed a nice guy, with a healthy approach to life and a great sense of humour. I must admit that I was impressed by his refinement and personal charm, but for me, the need to work together completely killed the desire to get into a romantic adventure with him.

Tuesday, 1 November

I slammed my alarm clock into silence with a heavy sigh. Today would have been mum's birthday. Again, I was met with the same dread that haunted me every morning for the past months since she passed away.

It used to be such a special day. I'd get up early and make her favourite Lincolnshire sausage sandwich, complete with an obligatory candle stuck in the middle, plus my morning coffee and her cup of tea. She would put on an act of surprise when I burst through her bedroom singing *Happy Birthday*. We would sit snuggled up in bed together, sipping our drinks while reminiscing about the year gone by and making plans for the next one.

Now, instead of sweet memories, all I tasted was bitterness and loneliness as I brewed myself a solitary cup of coffee. No more celebrating birthdays or making plans for the future. All that seemed so far away now, like a distant memory.

***

The tedium of the day took its toll on my already bad mood, yet I somehow got through all the braincell killing activities at work without any major psychological damage.

I raced home, hastily changing out of my office-appropriate attire and grabbed a bag that held the items I had prepped earlier that morning.

The cemetery was illuminated by dozens of tiny, twinkling lights, the sweet smell of freshly bloomed flowers hanging solemnly in the air.

I perched myself upon the bench beside the family grave, remembering the last time I was there with mum, when we visited my grandparents' resting place.

I held a white rose tightly in hand and gazed at the new inscription on the granite plaque.

The sight of so many silent graves surrounding me sent a shiver down my spine, not due to any spiritual feelings towards the dead, but rather because I was overcome with revulsion, that in these pits below lay countless bodies, slowly rotting away into nothingness. As always, it made me feel nauseous—today was no exception. I felt a sudden urge to flee this place and never look back.

I shut my eyes, my mind spiralling back five years ago when landing back home after a tearful cemetery visit, mum worked her magic to balance the world once again. I could already smell the coffee percolating in the kitchen and taste the cake she had baked earlier that day. On top of it all, there was the joyous soundtrack from *The Greatest Showman* thumping in the background.

'Hi!' I jumped, not expecting a presence in this quiet cemetery. My eyes were drawn to the figure beside me. It was John, looking right at her tombstone. My mouth opened and closed like a fish before I eventually gathered myself. 'John? What are you doing here?' I said flatly, raising an eyebrow.

He looked away from my mum's grave to answer me. 'Maya's birthday today and ... well, you weren't home, so I thought I'd find you here,' he said softly.

I sighed and shifted on the bench, feeling slightly overwhelmed by his sudden presence.

'First birthday without me,' I whispered with bitterness in my voice.

'Don't be sad, kiddo. Maya is no longer here. She's flown off to the nearest cloud, and she's probably sorry when she's looking at you now.'

'I can't help it. I miss her!'

'I know ... I know you do, kid,' he assured me and stroked my back with his hand. 'I went to visit Laura's grave today, and thought I would pop round for a cuppa on the way back home. And ask what's good.'

'Well, I got a new job.'

'In Moore Supplies?' he picked up.

'Yeah.'

'Fantastic!' He clapped his hands enthusiastically. 'You don't even know how happy I am for you!'

'Thanks,' I said, a little surprised by his joy. 'How did you get your hands on that job offer?'

'Uh ...' he mumbled and narrowed, obviously searching his head for some brilliant answer. 'I don't remember, to be honest ...'

'Harris, don't you lie to me.'

'I'm not planning to,' he admitted. 'So, we have to talk but not here.'

He walked over to the monument, ran his thumb over the golden letters that made up my mother's name and sighed.

'You are right. We need to talk,' I admitted humbly. 'I owe you an apology.'

I put a rose on a granite slab, right next to the candle that John lit.

'For what?' he asked, looking curious.

'For that Pentothal crap I was trying to pull off,' I said remorsefully. 'I don't know what came over me.'

'I'd like to know that as well,' he murmured. 'I can understand that you were losing patience with me, but I would never have accused you of such a stupidity.'

I cringed into myself. I was ashamed.

'Did you want to use these pills as a truth serum?' he asked, and when I gave him a nod of confirmation, he added, 'How did you even know that you can?'

'The work of an editor educates.' I laughed unhappily. 'I used to edit crime stories and I had to do quite detailed research ...'

'I guess I should start to fear what else you have learnt, editing true crime stories or horrors,' John said and tapped me on the shoulder.

'How did you know what I wanted to do with them?' I asked curiously.

'You divulged yourself.'

'Did I? How?'

'Any other time, you don't know how to shut your gob, and after returning with shopping, you were silent as if enchanted, and you crumpled something in your pocket ... When you took off your hoodie and put it on the bed, I decided to check what burnt your fingers so much.'

'But this powder could have been anything! How did you know what it was ...?'

He looked at me, shaking his head indulgently.

'You wrapped the crushed pills in the pharmacy receipt, you fool!' he explained mockingly. 'Almost all my life, I've had to be careful not to fall into some stupid traps. So, I shot you with your own weapon.'

'Yep, you sure did,' I admitted bitterly.

'Tough shit, kid,' he snorted and winked jokingly.

I breathed a sigh of relief. I didn't want to admit it to myself, but I missed Harris a bit. I felt stupid that I screwed everything up.

I took one last look at the grave, smiling in case my mother was actually watching me from a nearby cloud.

We left the cemetery. John put up the collar of his coat and lit his cigar.

'I parked right here. Come on, I'll give you a lift,' he offered. 'I'll have a cuppa with you before driving back home if you don't mind?'

'Sure, we have to talk as well ... don't we?' I asked hopefully.

He confirmed with a nod.

'Yeah, but let's do it inside, at home, without witnesses. When no one will hear your screams.'

'Screams? Why?'

'You will yell at me when you hear what I have to say to you.'

'Bloody hell, can't wait then ...'

***

I brewed a pot of tea and filled two cups with it. I handed one of them to Harris. I suggested moving to the couch in the living room. We sat at the opposite ends, covering our legs with warm blankets.

'Thomas Johnson is a fucking wanker, Lucy,' he said. 'You have to watch your back near him.'

'What?!' I almost spat out my tea.

I was sure I didn't tell him any details about my new boss. I just said I got a job.

'You have to watch your back, kiddo,' he repeated with concern in his voice and put the cup on the table.

'Wait, wait ... How ... how do you know him?'

'He's totally fucked up,' he interrupted me. 'Let me show you ...'

He thrust the green document folder onto my lap. I flicked it open, and a photo of a woman with a beaten face jumped out at me. It was as if Robert Helenius had taken a nasty seventh-round knockout from Anthony Joshua. Her lip was split and swollen, her eyes were blackened and heavy, and there was nothing but an icy void in her gaze. I was frozen to the spot.

'It's Hannah Johnson, the motherfucker's wife. She came to the Refuge about five weeks ago.'

'What the actual fuck!' I coughed up and covered my mouth with my hand. 'I don't understand a thing ... Yesterday Tom told me that his wife had left some time ago because they became strangers ... But wait, wait ...' I began to hastily flip through the contents of the folder. 'How could she find herself in a Single Mother's Home if they don't have children?'

'Did he tell you that?' There was contempt in John's voice. 'They have three kids.'

'Fucking liar!' I boiled.

'And a psychopath,' he added.

'I'm going to be sick,' I whispered and ran to the bathroom.

I turned on the tap, waiting for the water to get icy. I splashed it on my face several times. I couldn't believe what I had just learnt. It was a nightmare!

Harris turned me around and pulled me to him. I snuggled up to him and he patted me on the back reassuringly.

'You okay?' he asked.

'No, I'm bloody not okay!' I replied with a sigh. 'I'm sad.'

'It would be better if you were angry.'

'Why?!' I leaned back to look at him.

'Because anger drives people more to do something,' he replied. 'Sadness is the worst ally, I know it all too well.'

We returned to the living room. John put a cup of tea in my hands and covered my legs with a blanket.

'I don't get it,' I said, shaking my head. 'I just don't ...'

'I know. So now it's time for the part of the evening when you are really going to hate me,' he said, not looking at me.

'Great! Bring it on, like I don't have enough on my plate already,' I said ironically.

'After a few days of browsing through the folder with information about Johnson, I realised I couldn't go any further on my own. I had to find someone to help me get to him ...'

'And?' I murmured.

'I knew that because of what had happened in my home that night, I couldn't count on getting you on board. Knowing you, you were even more wired than I was.'

I didn't want to interrupt him, so I just rolled my eyes.

'During my investigation, I discovered that Johnson was looking for a new assistant ... I do not know what happened to the previous one, but an unusual opportunity has arisen. And with it, an idea, a wicked one, I must admit, but the only one that I came up with.'

'Right?!'

'It was because of me that you lost your job at the publishing house,' he blurted out, and I opened my mouth in indignation. 'I needed you at Moore Supplies. I had no other choice,' he added shamelessly.

'But how did you know where I worked?!' I choked out. He shrugged.

'I looked through the contents of your bag when you were in the cottage. You never know what's going to be useful to whom,' he said without a trace of remorse. 'I found your business card and found out what publishing house you worked for. In due course, I called the CEO to dazzle him with my alias and offer exclusivities for all the books I would write ... I even agreed to no advance payment. The only condition I gave him was that the staff should be reduced by your name ...'

'You fucking asshole!' I yelled, jumping from the couch. 'So, they fired me because of you?! You must be fucking joking!'

I walked around the living room like a wounded animal, cursing. Harris patiently waited for my outburst to end, but eventually, he could not stand it and said:

'Lucy, I just wanted to ...'

'I don't give a shit what you wanted!'

'Sit down, please. Let me explain.'

'No way!' I was raging. 'Don't tell me what to do. This is my house, and if I don't feel like sitting now, I'll stand!'

'Listen ...'

'What? Go on! What do you want to say?! That you meant well?! Your shitty tricks robbed me of the job I loved, you dickhead!' I was screaming so loud it hurt my throat. But I couldn't stop. 'Knowing that Johnson was a psycho, you pushed me into Moore Supplies. Straight into the lion's mouth! You're a fucking psycho too, you know that?!'

'Lucy ... I am really sorry,' he confessed. 'That's why I came to tell you everything ... My conscience gnawed at me.'

'Oh wow! Thank you! You are such a great man,' I mocked him, still fuming with anger.

I sauntered into the spacious kitchen and snatched a frosty bottle of Sauvignon Blanc from the fridge. I tilted my head back and guzzled the crisp liquid, feeling it swirl down my throat like a refreshing wave. Just as I reached for another helping, Harris slunk into the room, his face twisted with remorse. Despite his apologetic demeanour, I knew better than to trust him—after all, he was an expert at faking sincerity.

'Go ahead then, enlighten me with one of your famous quotations. I will forgive you instantly! After all, I'm just a silly girl who will dance to your tune! Come on!' I spat venomously, pouring myself a glass of wine.

He straightened up and, without a word, walked towards the door leading to the porch.

'Oh well done, mate! First wise decision today!' I complimented him sarcastically. 'See you never, you fu ...'

He drowned out my words by slamming the door.

I thudded the glass down and let out an enraged howl. My blood was boiling, my very being seething with injustice. I could feel salty tears streaming down my face as I leant against the sink, overcome with despair.

Suddenly, there was a noise at the porch door. Quickly, my head snapped up in fear. And there he was. John. Gripping a heavy crowbar and a hammer in his hands, with malice written all over his face. Instinctively, my arms flew to cover my barely-protected head, preparing for certain doom. The reality of death becoming increasingly real as I imagined what a fractured skull would look like splattered across the floor. My entire body seized with terror. 'You don't want to listen to me, maybe you'll listen to her,' he said, unusually calm for the circumstances, then he made his way to the hallway and stopped by the stairs.

After pushing the hammer behind the belt at the back of his trousers, he quickly slipped the end of the crowbar under the first step board and yank it open.

'Have you completely lost your mind?! What the hell are you doing?' I yelled, running up to him. I tried to hold his hand.

'Leave it, kid, I am warning you,' he said.

'I won't let you demolish my house, you psycho! Over my dead body!'

'Don't tempt me,' he gasped, pushing me away firmly with his free hand. I staggered.

I stood there gobsmacked, my eyes fixed on his movements. His rough hands moved swiftly and with precision as he dismantled the board of the first step. With a loud crack, it was removed from its hinges. He retrieved something from beneath the stairs—I couldn't make out what it was—and he placed it quietly by the wall. In an instant, he went back to restoring the damage he had caused earlier as if it hadn't happened at all. He even had a few nails in his pocket!

'Come on,' he said breathlessly when he finished.

I weighed up my options as he nervously stepped into the hallway and picked up the crowbar, hammer, and bundle. Taking a deep breath, I moved into the living room behind him with an overwhelming sense of dread.

My gaze fixated on the grey package tightly bound in a string that lay on the couch. Without warning, my hands began to shake as I unwrapped it—revealing a wooden box within. With a jolt, I realised there was something else inside: a memory stick!

My mind raced—what other secrets did this house hide?! Why didn't my mother tell me anything? Was she the one who hid the box? Suddenly, my spoonful of courage doubled, and I vowed to get to the bottom of this mystery once and for all.

'Gimme a laptop,' Harris said flatly without batting an eye at the discovery. I bit my lip and trudged off to fetch one as familiar feelings of unease swirled up in me like a whirlwind. He had some kind of mysterious power over me that made me queasy and uncomfortable beyond belief. It was as if I was surrounded by a hailstorm of secrets that were about to blindside me any minute.

John plugged the flash drive in and a few moments later, there she was—my mum, seated in the armchair in our living room, wearing a grey turtleneck jumper and looking like every ounce of life had been sucked out of her due to the illness. My chest seized up with grief as tears threatened to spill from my eyes. I couldn't help being reminded of all the happy days we used to spend together before her health deteriorated.

John hovered his finger above the play button and thrust the laptop closer to me.

'*Hi, birdy. If you're watching this, it means that my pre-departure plan has taken on the shape I wanted. I assume that neither of you decided to do a general renovation of the corridor (which I urge you to do at some point because our stairs are in poor condition), or Johnny needs help. I don't think this recording got out here by accident ...*' Mum smiled as if she was amused by her own words. '*However, I trust that the message I recorded would reach you at the right moment and that my words would bring you peace. Just in case, though, let me just say: Hi, Johnny!*'

She waved to us from the screen.

'Hi, hi,' Harris answered warmly, smiling back.

I wiped my tears with the cuff of my jumper. I reached for my laptop and placed it on my thighs. I wanted to have my mother closer to me. I didn't want to share her with anyone.

'Listen to me, birdy, we agreed with Johnny that he would show you this recording only when he believes it necessary. So, I assume that the time has come for my last request, amongst all the earlier ones of course. Do what he asks of you because he will never expect more from you than what you definitely will be able to handle. I'm sorry I never told you about this part of my life, and you had to find out about it that way. But I wanted to protect you from the violence and pain we've seen far too often. I know that John is not one of the most approachable people you will meet in life ... Need I say that you are not the only one who gets annoyed by his callousness and the fact that he is stubborn like a mule ... Johnny, if you hear this, do not frown. You know I'm right.'

Harris nodded with a single nod and spread his arms.

'Despite who he is, my lovely, one thing is for certain: you can trust him. Although how he works will not always be understandable to you, and you will probably disagree with his choices many times, know that this grump is a really good man with a heart of gold. Whatever you decide to do, honey, remember that I have always been and will be proud of you. You have given my life the deepest possible meaning. I love you, and I will continue to love you. Always and forever! Motherhood was the greatest adventure I've ever been on. I hope you will be able to

tell your child the same thing one day. Look after yourself. Remember that I will always be close. And you, John Harris, take care of my little girl and don't let anyone hurt her. You hear me? Because if you don't, I'll hunt your arse every night in your run-down cottage by the lake. I love you both. Until we meet again.'

The recording cut out and mum's face stayed frozen in the frame, her signature comforting smile lingering on my laptop. I couldn't take another second of seeing her, so I buried my face in my hands and let out a gut-wrenching sob.

'Come here, kid,' Harris whispered, pulling me close to him.

I couldn't resist snuggling into his arms and feeling the warmth of his deep embrace. We sank into each other for a moment before reluctantly dragging ourselves into the kitchen. I slumped down in a chair, hands cradling my weary head while he set about making coffee. With deft precision, he snapped on the spark arrester, and the gas burner came alive in a burst of flame. He effortlessly scavenged for the coffee and mugs from the cupboards as if it was something he had done many times before.

'We have things to talk about,' he said. 'Tomorrow, we have to start acting upon the plan ...'

'All right.' My mother's confidence was confined in my veins. I was capable but the fear of living up to her expectations crippled me. 'John, but what if I can't help?'

'You can and you will. I'll explain everything to you. Don't worry, kid.'

Wednesday, 2 November

Last night's conversation was more than just a discussion of details. John opened up to me and shared his story and the choices he had made that shaped his life now. With each tale, I began to understand why he felt it necessary to build a wall around himself. Not only was he terrified of being made a fool of due to his bad sight, but more so, he feared engaging with people who may one day uncover the secrets of his past.

Finally, I found out who the men who took Harris for a 'ride' that day were, and how they managed to find him. After Laura's death, which came unexpectedly, John lost the ground under his feet and went on a massive bender. A few days after his wife's funeral, as he was returning home from a pub, he got into a drunken fight with two men he met on the street. Unfortunately for him, it turned out that they were off-duty coppers. The initial scuffle quickly turned into a regular fight, as a result of which, one of the policemen landed in a nearby pond, the other jumped in to save him, and John legged it, losing his wallet with the driving license on the way. Before he managed to get home, the car had disappeared from the parking space near his house, and his apartment was demolished.

John spent the next three days at his friend's house opposite, watching his apartment from the window. When he was sure that he could safely return home, he packed whatever he felt necessary and disappeared. The apartment was emptied by a moving company and sold almost at once after putting it up for sale. He moved into an old cottage and probably would have managed to stay under the radar if I hadn't used his details when registering him at the optician's. The cops reacted quickly. The next day, they appeared at the cottage and took him for a revenge beating. Afterwards, they demanded money for the return of the car. John had a fondness for it because of Laura who a few years earlier had given him a Mercedes for his birthday. Harris managed to keep very few items accumulated during his life with her, so he decided to recover the car at all costs. He obediently paid the ransom and recovered the valuable keepsake.

After hearing this story, I understood why he reacted nervously to my suggestion of having an open conversation with the police about ways of helping the women of the Refuge. I also apologised to him for the trouble I had accidentally put him into. He forgave me. He explained that when I had asked about these men before, stupid male pride prevented him from admitting that he had behaved cowardly, running away like a rat from under a broom instead of facing them like the honourable man he thought he was.

I tossed and turned, unable to drift off all night. Harris was snoring away on the couch downstairs, an uncaring reminder of all the contempt I felt for what I was about to do. My conscience was in tatters, yet I had no choice but to go through with it. Hiding these motives felt like a fool's errand—I was never good at sugar-coating anything. But this time, the truth was far too dangerous to reveal.

***

My hurried morning commute was filled with pondering on the endless tasks that Harris had given me. He needed me to keep track of Tom's schedule for the next two weeks and somehow also find a way to get the keys to his family home.

Hannah's story left an unbearable ache in my chest, yet John warned me against being too sentimental about it. He reminded me that we had a cause to fight for and could not be sidetracked by emotions.

It was clear that Hannah needed our help quickly if she wanted to make any progress with her escape plan. It wouldn't be possible for her and the kids to access official systems, as they were without passports and any other necessary documents like birth certificates. She planned to take refuge with a family in France, though for now, that seemed impossible. I knew that we were her only lifeline and hope for escape.

***

I walked into the office building with a confident step, with the mask of a naïve assistant, blindly trusting her boss. I really wanted to do the job entrusted to me. However, I was afraid that due to my lack of experience and my bluntness, I could die along the way, getting John and Becky into trouble at the same time. I couldn't let that happen.

'Good morning,' I said cheerfully from the threshold of the office, but my expression grumbled when I saw the changed interior. 'What happened to the partition wall?' I couldn't hide my surprise.

'I asked the maintenance to dismantle it. I think it will be more convenient for us to work together without it. I hope you don't mind?' he replied and winked at me flirtatiously.

A shiver ran down my neck. Thinking that just two days ago I thought my new boss was a decent, trustworthy man made me sick.

'All right,' I said, though my hands were sticky with sweat.

I turned on my computer and looked at the messages in my mailbox. Then I checked the Outlook. The possibility of seeing Johnson's calendar would be very convenient for me. I decided to act right away.

'Tom?' I asked.

'Yes?'

'Could you share your calendar with me, please? It will be useful for planning your meetings and trips. I don't want to overlap a few things ...' I explained, without taking my eyes off the monitor.

'Sure, no problem,' he agreed. 'I'm sending it to you now. Let me know once you have access. You will have to update the calendar with several meetings.'

'Bingo,' I whispered.

'Got it?'

'Yes, I have been given permission to access it now,' I checked in.

'Great,' he said, handing me a few sheets. 'Here you go, my meeting-away timetable. Enter all these items into my calendar, please.'

'Of course,' I said, barely breathing with emotion.

'Are you feeling okay?' he asked concerningly. 'You look rather pale.'

'I'm just a bit hungover, I guess,' I said. 'Yesterday would have been my mum's birthday ...'

'Ah, right,' he reflected.

'I had a few drinks with a friend,' I grimaced in remorse to make my lie believable.

'Yes, that explains a lot,' he laughed and went about his desk.

I hastily tapped my boss's schedule into the calendar app on my phone, double-checking each entry against his overbearing gaze. I sent a copy to myself as well, just for an extra measure. The last thing I needed was for him to catch me snooping around and questioning his every move.

On the way home, I phoned John and informed him about my progress. He praised me and told me he would drop by on Saturday.

Friday, 4 November

The next two days were busy. I was put in charge of creating a new product brochure for the big conference. Johnson tried to come on to me, but I kept my cool. I knew he was getting frustrated with my lack of interest in him, so when I brought him coffee, I decided to tell him 'the truth'—that it was my first real assignment and that I didn't want to mess it up. It seemed to put him at ease, if only a little.

Friday afternoon was finally peaceful after Tom had left early, leaving me alone in the office. I rummaged through his drawers a bit, but there wasn't anything useful. Just before five o'clock, I emailed my presentation to Tom for approval before printing it and wished him a good weekend.

My mother was right—John wouldn't have given me the task if he thought I couldn't handle it. This gave me a small boost of courage.

***

I spent the evening in my mum's favourite armchair, dressed in soft plush pyjamas, wrapped in my favourite blanket. I had to relax after a few emotionally draining days.

I was drinking wine and reading about the funny adventures of the girls in *Steel Magnolias*, by Robert Harling, when my phone rang. An unknown number appeared on the screen. I answered, curious.

'Hello?' I said hesitantly.

'Hi, Lucy, you all right?' I heard Tom's voice. It sounded rather unofficial. 'Thank you for the file you sent.'

'There's nothing to be thankful for, boss,' I said hastily. My heart pounded with anxiety, and my breathing quickened. What did he want from me at this hour?

'Why so official, Lucy?' he asked. 'It's the weekend. It's time to chill out.'

'Thank you, I am very chilled. Are you okay with the brochure I have created?'

'Actually, that's why I'm calling ... I've found a few minor errors. Maybe I could drop by for a moment, and we'll figure out the details, huh?' he purred, and an unpleasant shiver ran down my spine at the sound of his words.

'Can't this wait until Monday morning?'

'I would prefer to close everything today and send the file to the printers as soon as possible. I will need these leaflets for Thursday's conference. And by the way ... I tried to change the booking so that you could go with me, but unfortunately, all the rooms have already been booked.'

Thank God! I thought with relief.

'So? I can pop round yours in an hour or so. Just give me your address,' he pressed.

'I'm so sorry, Tom, but I'm not home!' I lied. 'I'm at a friend's house, we're getting ready for a girls' spa trip ...'

I quickly turned on the TV with the remote control to disturb the silence in the house. It made me freeze to think that in the future Johnson could very easily access my address details. I didn't want to let him into my house, much less meet him alone.

'Eh, that's a shame,' he said with obvious disappointment. 'In that case, I will mark the file where the corrections should be made. You'll need to apply them on Monday morning. Good night and have a great weekend!'

'Thank you, and I am very sorry!' I replied, sticking to my story.

I ended the call and turned off the TV. I was overwhelmed with fear that he was watching my house from a safe distance. Maybe he was just checking me out ... This guy had no qualms. This was clearly shown by the image of his wife's mutilated face, which I could not erase from my memory.

Just in case, I decided to move with a book and wine to my bedroom. The windows of my room were not accessible from the street.

'*Take care of yourself. Remember that I will always be close,*' I remembered my mother's words. I felt another wave of sadness coming, so I poured wine into my glass and reached for the book. I fell asleep peacefully, relaxed by the funny adventures of the novel.

Saturday, 5 November

'Lucy! Get up, breakfast is almost ready!

'What about a coffee?' I shouted back, barely opening my sleepy eyes.

'Sure thing!' shouted Harris. 'Who do you think I am?!'

'An old grump!' I laughed.

'Come down, you cheeky mare!'

I rubbed my eyelids. I was not surprised by John's presence. At the end of his last visit, I decided to give him a spare key. I treated it as a symbolic proof of trust. I think that we both needed this gesture to continue our journey together.

I stretched out on the bed and kicked the covers off. When my nostrils picked up the smell of fried bacon, my mouth immediately filled with saliva. I didn't need extra encouragement to jump out of bed.

John was standing at the table with a plate and a mug in his hands.

'Scrambled eggs on toast and bacon, warm rolls with butter and coffee, my lady,' he recited, placing them on the table top. 'Just don't get used to it!'

'I wouldn't dare,' I said and nodded in thanks.

'Enjoy your meal. Eat before it gets cold.'

'Mmm,' I muttered with my mouth full.

John sat down opposite me with a book in his hand.

'What are you reading?'

'I'm finishing *On Writing: A Memoir of the Craft* by Stephen King. I like to go back to it from time to time to dust off the writing workshop,' he said openly.

'Nice,' I mumbled while munching. 'And how is it with ...'

'Didn't your mother teach you that you shouldn't talk with your mouth full?!'

'*Shorry*,' I said and swallowed a large bite, taking a sip of my coffee. 'Are you planning to write anything soon?'

'I'm getting ready, slowly but surely,' he admitted. 'But for now, my head is preoccupied with more important things, you know.'

'Sure. Speaking of important matters. Fire up my laptop. I'll show you what I got.'

'Hold your horses, kid. Eat up, get dressed, and then we'll have a look.' All of a sudden, he scolded me like a child.

'Okay, okay. Sorry, teach ... Food is delicious, thank you.'

'Course it is, I made it.'

After breakfast, I went back upstairs to do as I was told. I put on some jeans and a warm knee-length jumper. I tied my hair in a loose bun. When I went downstairs again, John was no longer in the kitchen. He sat on the porch, reading, wrapped in a cloud of cigar smoke. I made tea and joined him.

'Beautiful autumn this year, huh?' I noticed, handing him a cup.

'Yeah, nice and surprisingly warm,' he admitted. 'At least for now. It is supposed to cool down from Monday,' he added, closing the book.

'You know what worries me?'

'Winter?'

'No.' I shook my head. 'That I'll soon have to look for a new job again. I can't stay there, you know.'

'I know. Don't worry. You won't have to look for long. I'm sure of it.'

'Well, I hope so.'

'Did you ever think about working with publishing houses as a freelancer?' he asked, tilting his head.

'Somehow it never crossed my mind,' I said. 'But all in all, it makes sense to do so, I guess.'

He smiled in satisfaction as if he was glad I didn't turn his idea down.

'But don't worry about it for now, kid. There is work to be done first.'

'Should I turn on the laptop now?' I asked enthusiastically.

'Go on then.'

Soon, we both looked at my new boss's calendar.

'Johnson leaves for the conference on Thursday, early in the morning. For two days. I think it's a good opportunity to get what we're planning then. His next trip is scheduled in six weeks, see?' I pointed my finger at the right box.

'Okay,' John said emphatically, adjusting his glasses. 'It's doable but ...'

'I knew there would be a "but"!' I interjected impatiently.

'But to be able to enter his house, we have to have the keys, or we'll have to break in through the back door,' he explained. 'The problem is that he has an alarm installed.'

'And his wife doesn't have the keys?'

'Nope. She ran away from home in a hurry, remember?' I sighed.

'Okay, but she definitely should know the alarm code!' I suggested. 'And that's something, isn't it?'

'Yeah, but what if Johnson changed it?! We will be screwed if it goes off.'

'We?!' I asked gobsmacked.

'Well, yeah!'

'And what will you need me there for?!'

'Someone has to be standing as lookout, obviously.' I shuddered at the thought.

'Shit, my guts just knotted in my belly.'

'Don't panic, everything will be okay. I think later on we should visit Becky, talk to Mrs Johnson and ask about few things, so all will go smoothly.'

It somehow did not calm me down. Getting information is one thing, taking part in a burglary is a completely different matter.

'Why are you frowning?' he asked. 'Should I start worrying about you?'

'I just don't feel comfortable going there,' I replied honestly.

'That's understandable. However, there is work to be done, and I need your help, kid. So please help me.' John smiled and patted me on the shoulder. 'I don't have any more aces up my sleeve to convince you. I only have faith that you know what we are doing is a game worth playing.'

'Oh, for God's sake!' I rolled my eyes. 'Don't give me that look!'

'What look?!'

'The Puss in Boots look from *Shrek* ...'

'Who?!'

I looked at Harris as if he had dropped off the face of the earth.

'Don't tell me you've never seen it!'

'Nope,' he admitted, shrugging his shoulders.

'Your loss. If you had, maybe you could convince me to help you ...' I laughed.

'You are such a child sometimes!'

'And you are an old fart.'

'Eh.' He waved his hand. 'I'm going to get the phone from the car, and I'll give Becky a call and ask her to arrange for us to see Hannah.'

***

After the recent grand house clean-up just before Ginny's visit, I promised myself that I would never bring the place to such a state again. I guess I went from one extreme to another because now I kept cleaning like a madwoman. While waiting for Harris to return, I started washing the dishes. I was scrubbing the pan when he showed up in the kitchen.

'Ready?' he said.

'For what?' I asked, turning my head towards him. He looked very strange with unnatural eyes bulging, with his mouth bent corners downwards. 'Bloody hell!' I got scared, dropping the frying pan. 'Are you okay? Are you having a stroke?'

'What?! No! I'm making a face like that cat from *Shrek*,' he said grudgingly, putting his phone to his face, on which the appropriate picture from the film was displayed.

'You are a nutter, I swear to God,' I said, hardly restraining myself from laughing. 'Did you give Becky a ring?'

'Yeah, she will call us back in a few, and then we will talk to Hannah. Becky said that this woman had gone through such trauma that she does not want to see anyone face to face. Anyway, I guess it's for the best.'

***

Mrs Johnson's words confirmed John's assumptions. The alarm code at their house was updated every first day of the month, so it must have already been changed. But if we could get Tom's keychain and open the door with it, we'd have about thirty seconds to deactivate the alarm. The remote control in the form of a key ring hung in a box on the wall just behind the door in the hall. All it took was to press a button and the alarm would be disarmed without having to enter the code.

However, the operation seemed very risky. Eventually, Johnson could start carrying the remote control with him or move it to a completely different place. But let's just say we'd be lucky, and everything would go according to plan ... Except that you had to get the keys first. John claimed that guys usually keep their house and car keys in their pockets. I optimistically believed that Johnson used his coat pockets for this purpose. John laughed at me, saying that I was naïve and that such things only happened in bad TV series. We would have probably argued if the laptop hadn't pinged, announcing a new message in the mailbox. I clicked on the envelope in the corner of the screen, and a message from Johnson opened: *'Hello Lucy. Attached you findd the guidelines. Sorry I didn't do it yester day, but I got a cold. Make corrections att your free time and send back file overr. Thank you and best regards—Tom'.*

Judging by the number of typos, Johnson could indeed have been sick. Maybe he even had the man flu. A reckless idea formed in my mind. I knew it was dangerous, but the words tumbled out before I could stop them. If we could just get inside, maybe we could find the documents his wife needed. 'I have a plan!' I exclaimed.

'What plan?'

'Johnson has the flu,' I said happily.

'How do you know?'

'From the email, look,' I replied and showed him the screen.

'Right, and?'

'When a guy suffers from the man flu, you have to take proper care of him. After all, he is fighting for his life there! What kind of assistant would I be if I didn't take care of my boss in such a difficult time for him ...?'

'Do you want to go and see him?' he was worried. 'That's not a good plan, kid.'

'That's the only plan we've had so far,' I said. 'You said yourself that we have to act quickly.'

'That doesn't mean you have to hurl yourself into his grasp. He's a dangerous man!'

'You made me work with him in the first place,' I reminded him acerbically. 'Come on, let's go!'

'We can't! Haven't you told him last night you were going to spend the day at the spa?' he protested weakly.

'I'll figure an excuse when it comes to it,' I said, and I got up from the couch, gesturing for him to do the same. 'You do know his address, don't you?'

He confirmed with a slight tilt of the head.

'There is no time to waste,' I said, putting my laptop in my bag. 'We have to grab some food on the way ...'

My heart raced as the car pulled up to the outskirts of town. I knew that what we were about to embark on was madness, but it was a risk worth taking. I ordered a leek and potato soup and steak pie combo from the restaurant on the way. As we came closer to Tom's hometown, all my doubts began to surface. My palms were sweaty with apprehension as if I knew that this plan would be more difficult than I anticipated. I took a deep breath, reminding myself why I was doing this in the first place. I mustered up my courage and prepared for whatever fate awaited me.

'Don't forget for a split second why you're there,' John said in a choked voice. 'Keep your guard up, be careful. Understand?'

'I know.'

'It was a lot easier to do some things to some people back in the day,' he noted. 'People rarely had cameras, alarms, or other inventions in their homes.'

'So maybe it's time to think about retirement ...' I grumbled under my breath.

'This is probably not the best time for that sort of conversation, don't you think, kid?' he cut in, looking carefully at the road and turning into Johnson's street. 'We're here ... I'll park around the corner at the end of the road. If the situation starts to get out of control, call me right away. You don't have to say anything, just dial my number and I'll come round in a flash.'

'All right,' I agreed, keeping Harris's number on speed dial. 'Let's just hope it won't come to that.'

John parked his car by the curb, just before turning off the street where Johnson's house was. He pulled his phone out of his pocket and placed it on his lap. Seeing it made me feel a bit safer. I took a deep breath and then grabbed my laptop bag and the bag of food.

'See you in a minute,' I said, reassuringly. 'Keep your fingers crossed.'

'Be careful, kid.'

I strode towards Johnson's front garden, my hand hovering above the bell button at the entrance gate. With a jolt, the sound of unlocking blared from the intercom, and I threw open the gate. The crunch of gravel beneath my feet echoed eerily as I made my way up the stone pathway.

The house was average-sized—not huge but certainly flashy enough to give away its owner's wealth. A light cream façade gleamed in the day, contrasting with dark ceramic tiling framing the gable roof and wooden shutters adorning each window. The garage nearby had an ajar door that revealed a sleek Land Rover parked within. Everything made a very pleasant impression. Probably no one could have guessed the drama taking place behind the doors of this house.

When I went to the door, I put the bag of food in my other hand and knocked hard with the brass knocker. Soon Johnson stood in the doorway. He looked nothing like that cute guy I met at the greasy spoon that day. He was dressed in a short black dressing gown, not even reaching the middle of his thighs, casually tied with a belt. The parted halves exposed part of his bare chest. At the very sight, I felt sick, and soon I also smelt the unpleasant mix of alcohol and sweat.

'What are you doing here?' he mumbled. He was clearly wobbling on his feet. He leaned his whole body against the doorframe. 'Should you not be at the spa?'

'Hi, boss. Unfortunately, we had to postpone,' I said, not showing surprise at his condition. 'I received your email and decided to check how you are. I brought a home-made dinner. Can I come in, please?'

'Sure thing ...!' he said contently, standing away from the doorframe and gesturing me into the corridor. I thanked him with a smile. 'Welcome to my home!'

Adrenaline coursed through my veins like crazy because I realised I had to put all eggs in one basket. Another such opportunity may not happen again. I entered the living room and stood next to the table near the couch. His countertop was covered with a half-drunk bottle of vodka, a bottle of body lotion, and crumpled tissues scattered everywhere.

'Apologies for the mess,' he muttered, slamming his laptop shut with force. I had caught a glimpse of a vulgar still from an adult film before he closed it. 'The flu has me bedridden.' I perched myself on the corner of the sofa, producing the takeout containers I had picked up on my way over.

'I hope you fancy some soup and pie,' I said with a smile. 'You have to eat to get well.'

He spread his hands as if to say that if I thought so, he would accept.

'Good, in that case, you just lay down and rest, and I'll heat it all up for you,' I said. 'I'll find the kitchen!'

'You really are fantastic!' he noted, sitting on the sofa. He leaned back on it, and I covered him with a blanket I found on the chair.

'That's what you have assistants for, isn't it?' I said, winking flirtatiously.

'I'm a lucky son of a bitch,' he praised as I left the room.

I put the food containers on the kitchen counter and pulled my phone out of my jumper pocket.

Jonhson is pissed. I'm heating up his food. I'll text you when I can open the back door. No cameras downstairs.

I sent a message, then went through the cabinets for suitable dishes. When I found them, I put the soup in the microwave.

I slipped off my shoes to silently head back to the living room and see what the host was doing. He was still covered with the blanket, still in the same position I had left him a moment ago.

'Tom, are you asleep?' I whispered.

'No,' he mumbled without opening his eyes. 'I'm just resting my eyes and waiting for you.'

'The soup is nearly ready. Just a minute. Could I use your toilet, please?'

'Sure. First door on the left, past the stairs.'

'Okay. Do you want to have some water or tea?'

'No, thank you,' he denied in a weak voice.

I walked through the hall, passing by the staircase and security system. Ah, there it was— the box that Hannah had mentioned, packed with keys, including one for the back garden. I quickly used the restroom, washing my hands furiously under a torrent of water.

I reached for the backdoor handle, unlocking it with a twist of the key. I opened it as quietly as possible—only to be greeted by the sudden beep of the microwave announcing dinner was ready. To the right of the door, I noticed an office—Johnson's likely hiding place for important documents. No time to investigate now. I needed to make it to the kitchen before Johnson woke up.

I grabbed the bowl of soup from the microwave and then stuffed the pie inside. 'Tom, dinner is served,' I called out as sweetly as I could manage, setting down the bowl on the table.

Johnson jolted awake at my voice, gazing around in confusion before finally resting his bleary eyes upon me and smiling at his soup. He pulled himself into a chair across from me, and we settled in for dinner.

'It smells beautiful. Did you cook yourself?' He started to eat without waiting for my answer.

'No, I bought it,' I said bluntly. 'Enjoy your meal!'

At the sight of soup dripping down his beard, I felt sick again. He slurped it like a dog. At some point, he moved closer to the table. The short dressing gown opened, revealing that he was completely naked underneath. I immediately associated what connected the porn in the laptop, crumpled tissues, and lotion. It was hard for me to hide my disgust for this man, so I went to the kitchen to get the pie out of the microwave.

Johnson ate it all, wiped his greasy lips with the back of his hand and burped loudly.

'You have a beautiful house,' I said. 'Very tastefully decorated.'

He nodded, accepting the compliment with satisfaction.

'And it's massive!'

'Two floors?' I enthused. 'I'd love to see the rest ... Could you show me around, please?'

I smiled flirtatiously. Johnson gave me a strange look. I couldn't decipher his expression. I was frightened that he saw through me, even though he could not have known my intentions.

'Sure! Come on then,' he said, rising from the chair with difficulty.

I took the dirty dishes to the kitchen. Tom was waiting for me on the first step of the stairs, holding on to the wall with one hand and squeezing the railing with the other. He moved slowly, staggering step by step. I walked right behind him, writing out a message to John in a hurry.

Come in. Back door. We are upstairs. Office first door to the right.

'I decorated the whole house myself,' he mumbled with undisguised pride. 'With my hard-earned money! I like luxury.'

'You have great taste. I'm impressed.'

We reached the first floor. Tom opened the first door on the right. The room we found ourselves in was probably the main bedroom. Although I did not notice any small things that his wife would leave here, the wallpapers and decorative accessories indicated a woman's taste. I realised that the window overlooks the part of the garden where John should appear soon. I had to distract Johnson somehow.

In an act of desperation, I put my hands on his shoulders and turned him gently towards me. I whispered in his ear the first words that came to my mind:

'Do you often hit the gym? You look like you're in great shape ...' I said, trying to distract him.

He raised his arms and flexed his biceps with pride as he murmured, 'I like to keep in shape. See anything else you like?' He then reached for my wrist and slipped it over his bulging crotch underneath his dressing gown.

I jumped back in shock, trying to distance myself from him and stumbling frantically to the window, feigning interest in the view outside. But Johnson didn't let up; he immediately clamped onto me from behind, wrapping one arm around my neck tightly. The panic set in; my heart raced as I struggled to breathe shallowly. Just as I felt Harris would appear at any given moment, confusion swamped my mind.

'Didn't you like what you found there, baby?' he growled and licked my ear. 'I know you want it.'

A thousand thoughts crossed my mind. I was afraid. I knew what he was capable of. Alcohol and impetuous were an extremely dangerous mixture. To think that

I got into this crap at my own request! But I wasn't going to give up easily. I decided to put on a brave face and start taking control of the mess I had got myself into. I couldn't suddenly start screaming for help. My screams would probably only arouse more aggression in this psycho.

Anyway, I had a job to do.

Despite the disgust that Tom's touch filled me with, I decided not to resist, giving him a sense of control over the situation. I tilted my head back, resting it on his shoulder. I pressed my butt against his lower abdomen. I could feel his excitement.

'I loved it,' I assured him. 'And I want more, much more, boss.'

'I like the sound of that,' he replied, freeing me from under his grasp.

He firmly turned me to face him and with a theatrical gesture untied the strap of his dressing gown, exposing his naked body. I shoved my trembling hands into my jeans pockets and bit my lip as a sign that I liked what I was seeing.

I didn't know what would happen next. I prayed for deliverance. Then, out of the corner of my eye, I saw a leather belt hanging on a hook on the back of the door. Without thinking, I pushed him, leading him backwards towards the bed. He did not protest. He smiled as I rested my hands on his shoulders and pushed him to sit on the edge of the bed.

'Since this will be our first, and hopefully not the last time, I think we should have some proper fun,' I said as bossily as I could imagine. 'What do you say?'

Johnson looked down at his hard penis and purred, smiling. Without letting him out of my sight, I removed the strap from the hook and slammed it into the sheets right next to his thigh. He hissed excitedly and lay on his back, clutching his nipples with his fingers. He looked pathetic.

I sat astride him and bound his hands at his wrists until he grunted unconsciously. Then I put the end of the strap through the metal frame of the bed and pulled with all my strength so that he did not have too much room for manoeuvre.

'I knew you liked to have fun from the moment I saw you that day at the café,' he mumbled, giving me complete control over him.

'Well. You are an expert on women, aren't you ...'

'I wish my fucking wife liked to have so much fun,' he murmured, sticking out his tongue disgustingly.

His words went straight through me like an electric shock.

'Fucking wife?!' I spat through gritted teeth. My vision blurred with rage, and my fists were clenched tight, my heart pounding faster than ever before.

The first punch connected with his nose, the second cutting open his lower lip. I couldn't stop, throwing punches even as the pain from my knuckles began to resonate up my arm. Johnson seemed stunned and confused—perhaps he'd taken my heated words as a sign of reconciliation. But then the blood began to gush onto the pristine white sheets on the bed, and he yelled in agony. His screams only spurred me on further. I continued to hit him, over and over again, everywhere I could reach. His body thrashed like a fish out of water.

At one point, unfortunately for me, he managed to break one of his hands free and pushed me back with enough force that I lost my balance and fell to the floor with a sickening thud, radiating pain from my ribs. At that moment, it clicked what every woman who has felt the onslaught of an abuser must have felt—pure hatred mixed with terror and helplessness. The red mist returned to my eyes, and instinctively, I reached out for the metal candlestick on the dresser next to me. He tried kicking out at me again, calling me names, and threatening to finish me off once and for all. And so, I swung ...

'What the actual fuck?!' I heard a roar right behind me. I span around and saw Harris, his face reddened with rage. The force of his fury was so overwhelming that I felt my energy drain away from me as if it were being sucked out of me. I dropped the candlestick and crumpled to my knees as a sharp pain seared through my left side, piercing like a knife. Groaning in agony, I looked up but couldn't make sense of what I was seeing. All I could focus on were John's hands, stained red with blood.

The sheets were drenched in a crimson hue, and Johnson was shaking uncontrollably. Red foam bubbled out of his mouth as Harris placed a pillow across his face.

'Don't look,' he demanded.

Swallowing hard, I grasped onto the bed frame and tried to stand up without success; every ounce of strength had been sapped from my body.

'I said don't fucking look at him!' His voice boomed like thunder. Trembling, I bent down and stared at my hands—they were mysteriously spotless.

'John ...' My voice broke into a whisper after a few moments of stillness. 'I don't know ... I don't know what happened ...'

He came over to me and lifted me off the ground before pulling me close into an embrace. 'You lost control,' he mumbled softly into my neck. As I inhaled his familiar scent, I asked the question that had been burning inside my chest: 'Did I kill him?'

'No ... You didn't kill him,' Harris replied.

'But he's not moving!' My voice came out high-pitched and panicked.

'He fainted from the pain. We gave him a good walloping, that's all,' Harris said grimly. He urged me to go downstairs and wait for him while he returned to the room. I did as he instructed, trembling with fear at what I had got myself into. What would the consequences of this mess be?

Still sobbing, I barely heard Harris's footsteps as he descended the staircase. He placed his hands on either side of my face and looked deep into my eyes; his gaze was so intense it stopped me in my tracks.

'Lucy, now is not the time for tears. You have to stay focused and think back to when you arrived here—every step you took, everything you touched,' he insisted firmly. 'We need to figure out our story before anyone else does.'

I swallowed hard as I closed my eyes and tried to recall each moment I'd experienced since arriving at the house earlier in the day. As soon as I began speaking, Harris whipped out his phone and jotted down my answers: 'The gate bell, the knocker on the door, the couch armrests ... and a million other things in the kitchen!'

'Fuck's sake!' Harris groaned in frustration. 'What were you thinking?'

'John ... How are we going to explain this beating up?' I cried, wiping away tears.

'There's no "we," kid. You were never here,' he replied coolly.

'What?'

'It's not the beating that needs explaining, it's the aftermath. Don't worry about it,' he said emotionlessly, passing me his phone. 'Don't panic, Blackbird! No tears,' he warned, gripping my shoulders tightly. 'Look at me when I speak to you.'

I peeled my hands away from my face.

'Is he ...'

'Yes.'

'And I ...?'

'No, not you. It was all me.' He squeezed my shoulders again before pressing his forehead against mine for a moment. 'Calm down and breathe,' he instructed firmly. I inhaled deeply through my nose and exhaled slowly through pursed lips. 'Again,' he urged me, and with each breath, my racing heart slowed to a steady beat.

'Now write down everything you have touched here on my phone, one by one. Focus, it's important.'

I mentally retraced my steps and carefully documented every detail. When I finished, I handed the phone back to Harris.

'Right, take my car, get home pronto, and have a shower. Chuck the clothes you're wearing in the fireplace and burn them. Then reply to Johnson's email and wish him well, adding that you'll pick up the corrections Monday morning.'

'I can do it now. I've got my laptop with me,' I said and pointed to the bag in the living room.

'Better to do it from home, kiddo. In case anyone bothers to check the IP address of the mail, at least it won't lead back here. Worst case scenario, and all that.'

'Okay then.'

'Afterwards, go see Becky and let her know what's happened, no need for details ...' he continued before I had a chance to ask about himself again. 'I'll sort out erasing any trace of us being here and then try to work out what comes next. Oh, and act normal—you know, like nothing shady went down, alright? Chances are you'll be at work as usual on Monday morning, so don't give anything away, no matter what.'

My chest tightened, and my eyes clouded over once more. 'What if something goes wrong?'

He grinned confidently, 'Everything's going to be peachy, kid, this ain't my first rodeo! Now chin up!'

I shook my head in dismay. What a bloody mess this was turning into!

John shrugged nonchalantly, 'Shit happens, but we'll get through it somehow. Don't worry about me by the way, just look after yourself, yeah?'

'What about your car?'

'Leave it at the Co-op car park on Stamford Road, love. The key's under the right front tyre. Don't call me. I'll contact you.'

I nodded reluctantly, trying not to let my fear show through my face. I didn't want John to go alone, but he wouldn't have it any other way. He pushed a bag into my hands and then kissed my forehead goodbye.

The drive home felt like an eternity—but when I finally got there, I had to act quickly. I sanitised the steering wheel and door handle with a hand sanitiser and put the key where he'd asked me to. Then I raced home, stripped off the clothes that I'd been wearing and burnt them all in my garden firepit, even the coat! After taking a long hot shower, I sat down to answer Tom's email exactly to John's instructions, without shedding a single tear. Obediently, I followed his instructions like a mindless robot; anything to please my mentor.

With little time to spare, I jumped into my car and raced to meet Becky at The Refuge, hoping she'd be there. Now more than ever, I needed to be strong—for Harris's sake.

The huskie-voiced woman recognised me straight away and asked if I was okay to find Becky's office myself. I confirmed and thanked her for the help. I walked down the corridor, arranging in my head what I was going to say to Becky.

The whole purpose of the visit to the Johnsons' house was to find the documents, which would enable the abused wife to take refuge with her children with a family in France. Meanwhile, I returned empty-handed. Even if we could easily find the children's ID cards and birth certificates and take them out of the house, the fact that Hannah had them in this situation and the tragic death of her husband could direct the suspicions of the police to her. It was safer not to take anything. Mrs Johnson regained her freedom with the death of her husband. She didn't know it yet, but she had just become a widow. She could decide for herself about her life and that of her children.

Becky sat quietly at her desk as I told my story, unfazed by the situation—after all, this wasn't her first rodeo either. She listened thoughtfully before pulling out a piece of paper and jotting down some information.

'Are you injured? Is something wrong with you?' she asked.

'No.'

'And Johnny?'

'No.'

'That's good.'

'But Johnson isn't ...!' It broke out of me. And as much as I tried to control myself, I felt my jaw tremble.

She nodded in understanding as if she knew what I was thinking.

'Do you want to stay with me?' she proposed calmly. 'I'm nearly done for the day.'

'No. I need to go home,' I decided, though her proposal was tempting. 'John told me to behave normally. I'm supposed to go to work on Monday and pretend I don't know anything. No matter what ...' I recited Harris's words mechanically. 'And tomorrow, I'll sleep all day.'

I left without saying goodbye. I got in the car and drove off home.

I have no idea how I didn't cause an accident on the way back. I was driving on autopilot. During the ride, I accompanied myself with the irrational thought that if I managed to go home and sleep in my own bed, it would erase all the terrible images from my head.

Monday, 7 November

My hopes of sweet dreams were in vain. I had been wrestling with my demons for two sleepless nights, and this day just seemed to drag on forever. I finally dozed off, but not long after awoke in a panic with the images of Tom's bedroom flashing through my mind.

It felt like a heavy fog was hovering above me until it consumed me completely. No matter how much I ate or drank, I still tasted the bitter, metallic tang of fear on my tongue.

In desperation, I got out of bed with my heart pounding and ran into the shower, deluding myself that the stream of hot water and soap would wash away the viscosity and weight I felt. But no amount of scrubbing could take away the feeling of inertia that persisted inside me. No tears would come either, though I wanted to scream and cry my heart out.

As the morning inched closer, I found myself leaning against the headboard, staring out into the darkness. When the cockerel heralded Monday, I almost screamed out loud. My heart raced just thinking about it—John, Becky, and Johnson. The guilt nagged at me. After all, this was entirely my fault for even suggesting we go there that day.

I've been replaying the scenes of the last few days in my head endlessly since I showed up at the cottage at the edge of the forest, less than two months ago.

I got out of bed when the alarm went off. After a sleepless night, I didn't have the strength to go to work, but I knew that I had to do everything according to John's instructions. I couldn't let him down. I had to grin and bear it, show up on time in the office, and act as if nothing had happened.

I tumbled into my grey pencil skirt and black jumper, pulling the sleeves over my tender knuckles. To my relief, no bruises revealed themselves; all signs pointed to me having thrown softer punches than I'd thought. At least there was no evidence of the incident for me to hide at work—that would have been far too difficult. I quickly swept my hair into a loose braid and touched up my makeup, masking any trace of fatigue from my face. It was time to battle through another day.

I was determined to take a detour and see for myself if the Mercedes was still there. My heart sank as I noticed the empty parking spot. I felt my hand continually reach for my phone, desperate to hear John's voice and know how he fared in his negotiations. Yet, I wasn't sure if I should call him after his request not to. Despite the need to pick up the phone, I restrained my trembling fingers—if only to show him that much respect.

***

As I strutted towards the entrance of the office building, I heard familiar voices. My colleagues were moaning about the usual Monday blues and lack of weekend options. I tweaked my expression to a polite smile before walking into the lift with Charlie. He requested me to send him the final version of the company's new leaflet, so he could work his magic on the design. I gave him a blunt nod as a promise, and he replied with a jokey wink that I should make sure no typos slip through this time.

I heaved a sigh of relief as I entered my office, grateful to be alone with my thoughts—thankful I no longer had to pretend that everything was alright. My gaze naturally gravitated towards the empty chair at Tom's desk, sucking any lingering energy out of me until all that was left was raw vulnerability. Taking a deep breath,

I flicked on my computer and started going through each line of text in the promotional leaflet one by one—it was almost certain that I would miss something crucial while feeling a little less than composed. Just as I was about to hit 'send' on Charlie's email, Michael Moore popped his head around the edge of my doorframe.

'Good morning, Lucy,' he greeted me cheerfully, then pointed to Johnson's empty desk. 'Thomas not in yet?'

'I don't think so, I haven't seen him yet,' I replied, involuntarily hiding my hands under the desk.

'Strange. He was supposed to come and see me in the morning to discuss the details of the conference,' he said and pulled his phone out of his jacket pocket.

'On Saturday, I got an email from him saying he had a cold. Maybe he didn't feel well enough to work today ...?' I suggested.

'Hm. His phone is off,' Moore said, scratching his head. 'It's not like him to pull a sick day, he must have got really poorly,' he concluded. 'I'll drive up to him on the way to the meeting, it's on my way. I'll check how he is.'

'Good idea, boss,' I said, smiling. 'That's very nice of you.'

'We've been working together for over ten years willy––nilly. We got close. And, as you probably know, man flu is no joke!' he joked and left.

My heart was racing as I felt the cold beads of sweat trickling down my temples and neck. I was so over-whelmed that I could barely see through my tears. My body trembled, and every muscle contraction sent excruciating pain shooting through my tender ribs. With a lurch, I threw up in the bin beside me, and the acrid smell of vomit filled the room. I gritted my teeth, grabbed the bin, and headed to the bathroom at the end of the hallway.

I glared at my reflection in the bathroom mirror. I'd hoped that the foundation and mascara would've given me some extra radiance, but it only made me look paler and more worn. Wiping away the smudge of tears and makeup with a tissue from my pocket, I filled my hands with cold tap water and gulped it down.

Back in my office, I opened the window wide—an act of rebellion against the stifling air-conditioning. All too aware of the tranquillisers tucked away in my purse, I decided to numb my guilt with medications. A few minutes later, I brewed myself a comforting, yet potent blend of lemon balm tea. After about twenty minutes, the drug and sedative herbs began to work. The trembling of my hands and the sweat that washed over me stopped, and the pulse rumbling in my temples died down enough that I could focus on work. I read the brochure for Charlie again and sent him the corrected file. I replied to a few emails. I filled out an additional form for human resources.

My heart leapt into my throat as the footsteps in the hallway thundered closer. I imagined a swarm of police officers storming through the door, ready to haul me off for murder.

My fingers trembled against the edge of the desk as the doorknob creaked with a menacing rattle. I was alone, and yet I felt more exposed than ever before.

'Boo!' exclaimed Charlie, amused by my expression. 'You look like you've seen a ghost!'

'Don't be daft,' I murmured.

'I came round for a chat, 'cause I heard in the kitchen that Tom took a day off today. I decided to keep you company for a while because you must be terribly bored. See what I brought you. Healthy orange juice for a good start to the week.'

'That's very nice of you. Thanks.' I smiled, reaching out for a glass.

'No problem, I have to suck up to you somehow,' he said with a feisty face.

'Why?' I asked, surprised.

'I sent you the finished file for approval. Take a look with your professional editorial eye to see if there is any crap left there.'

'Crap?'

'Yes ... Typos and other things.'

He was adorable. He came and made me laugh, not even knowing how much I needed a moment of normality.

We went through the document together, scrupulously checking every detail of the text and graphics. Once everything was in order, I sent an email to Tom asking him for his official approval. Anyway, that's what I was instructed to do during my training.

Charlie invited me out for lunch at the local greasy spoon. I almost declined at first because the location reminded me of Tom. But then I agreed—after all, I needed to pretend that life was still going on as normal. Plus, most of our colleagues would usually have something to eat there during their lunch break.

We secured a cozy corner by the luminous window and ordered some burgers with cheesy chips. As I savoured each bite, I felt my hands tremble involuntarily once again. Without hesitation, I retrieved another pill from my purse and swallowed it, explaining that I occasionally use medication to deal with the grief of losing my mother. This sparked a heart-to-heart conversation about our respective families and loved ones. To my surprise, Charlie divulged that he had also lost his mother to cancer just a few years prior, which helped to strengthen our connection.

As we walked back to the office building, Charlie turned to me and asked an unexpected question. 'Lucy ... do you like working with Thomas?'

'Yeah, I guess so,' I said.

'He's not hitting on you yet?' I stopped, surprised by his words. 'Cause you know ... Rumours have it that his previous assistants resigned from their jobs because ... How to put it politely ...? He couldn't keep his hands off them,' he explained, floundering. 'I've heard he's a bit of a perv.'

I shook my head in indignation.

'You said a few days ago that he was a pretty cool guy!'

He was visibly confused. 'But then I had a slightly different opinion of you.'

'Meaning?'

'I was still a bit mad at you for grassing me up to the boss like that. I thought that you were full of it.'

'And now?' I asked offensively.

'And now I don't think so,' he said, smiling innocently. 'You're a good girl. So, watch out for yourself, okay?'

'I'll try.'

'And if he starts hitting on you, I will come to the rescue. Well, unless ...'

'Unless what?'

'Unless you like it, then I won't come to the rescue.'

'I can assure you that I won't in the slightest. You can come and save me anytime,' I said amused.

'Okay then. In that case, I shall come to your rescue anytime you call, my lady!'

'My hero!'

We enjoyed our chitchat so much that we didn't even realise that we got back late from lunch.

'Thank God you're both back. I was looking for you everywhere!' said a breathless Fiona Green when we came out from the lift. 'Michael has called an urgent staff meeting in the conference room. Let's go!'

My heart started pounding like crazy. I knew what we were about to hear. I entered the conference room on soft legs. The room was stuffed with people. There was an incredible buzz here. Surely everyone wondered what happened. Charlie pointed to an empty chair and stood behind me, leaning against the wall. Fiona pushed her way through the throng of people, loudly demanding their attention. When all movements stopped and everyone's gaze locked on her, she stood tall and said in a sorrowful yet commanding voice: 'I am terribly sorry to announce that our beloved co-worker Thomas Johnson has passed away tragically ...' The collective gasp echoed off the walls of the room as Fiona continued her address with deep regret in her tone.

At the sound of her words, several women burst into tears, and my body went numb because my mind was already aware of the irreversibility of what had happened last Saturday. I involuntarily pulled the sleeve of my jumper over my hand and covered my mouth with it, holding my breath. Charlie, seeing this, put his hand on my shoulder.

'I don't have many details about this tragedy so far. Mr Moore is still at the scene talking to the police,' Fiona continued in a trembling voice, barely holding the tears back. 'The management has decided to shorten today's working day in this extraordinary situation, so you can go home. Tomorrow, we start at the normal time.' That said, she left the room accompanied by other board members.

It got loud again. People reacted differently: some were silent, shaking their heads in disbelief, others showered each other with questions and various speculations about what had happened.

Charlie squeezed my arm again, this time encouraging me to leave.

'Do you want me to stay with you?' he asked with concern already in the corridor.

'No, thanks,' I replied. 'I would like to digest this news alone ...'

'All right. Here you have my business card,' he said, shoving a narrow card into my hand. 'Call me when you want to talk, okay?'

I agreed and hurried to my office. I closed the door and cried again. This time they were not tears of fear or despair—rather relief that everyone already knew that Johnson was dead.

***

I had nothing planned for the afternoon, but I knew I didn't want to be cooped up in my house by myself.

I gave Becky a ring and after the usual pleasantries, I asked if she'd spoken to John recently. She said she'd tried calling him, but it went straight to his voicemail—he hadn't replied to any of her messages either. Instantly sensing my apprehension, she sought to reassure me that this wasn't an uncommon occurrence. It seemed as though there was something deeper beneath the surface, yet we both knew that discussing it further would be futile over the phone.

All I could really do was grab my car keys and go.

***

As I strolled around the cottage, an eerie silence engulfed me. The sun was setting, and it felt as if nothing had been disturbed in a while, except for John's beloved car was gone. I rapped on the door, but there was no answer—only a sorrowful echo bouncing off the walls. I tried turning the handle but soon realised it was locked shut. So instead, I looked through the window for a glimpse inside. It seemed the house had been cleared out of all furnishings—his bookshelf, chest of drawers and armchair were nowhere to be seen—except for a small table with chairs and a roll of burgundy carpet by the bedframe, which lacked a mattress and quilt. As the shadows grew, a sense of foreboding filled my stomach.

I pondered where Harris had vanished without a trace, taking all his possessions. I reached the pear tree, wondering if something had been altered here—John would certainly have dug up his treasure chest if he was intending on escaping. The earth was disturbed—he hadn't even bothered to cover it back up with leaves and soil. An abandoned spade rested nearby, implying he'd left in haste.

My footsteps echoed along the familiar path, taking me closer to the lake. I stopped short when I reached it, my heart fluttering at the sight of a freshly engraved inscription on the backrest of the bench. 'CHIN UP.' Tears filled my eyes as I realised this was John's doing—a sweet and thoughtful gesture from one friend to another. I felt an overwhelming rush of emotions, and in that moment, I knew that everything would be alright.

The sky was dimming, and I wrapped my woollen jumper tighter around myself. As I sat on the bench facing the lake, I noticed that while the autumn clouds created a muffled darkness, beneath them, the lake and trees remained serenely still. Closing my eyes, I allowed myself to bask in nature's tranquil melody. With a heavy heart, I said farewell to this place—it had been an intense but brief chapter of my life.

As the sky blushed a deep pink, I returned to the cottage, where my car was parked. Still searching for Julian, but to my relief, he seemed to have gone with John.

One last look at the now empty house brought a pang of loss, although nothing actually belonged to me. With each step away from it, a feeling that something had been taken, yet again, seemed to linger.

I had returned to my hometown broken-hearted, only to find two words carved into the bench. I treaded home, forlorn. When I arrived, a piece of paper jammed under the door caught my eye, and I rushed forward. Hands trembling, I peered at the page in my phone's light—John's swansong.

I had to go. You know I did, at least until things die down. We are going to settle somewhere nice with Julian. You'll be safer away from me, though it is with a heavy heart that I write this. As a farewell, I will entrust you with the last task: let yourself fall in love, kiddo. Not every relationship is doomed to failure—remember that. So go and fall in love, okay? I promise it's worth it! And let yourself be loved. Believe me, you will like it.

A year later

'How's my girls?' he greeted me when I went down to the kitchen.

'Mmm,' I murmured sleepily, coming closer and kissing him on the lips.

'I knew you slept well because you didn't fidget much and didn't talk in your sleep,' he said, then knelt in front of me and brought his face close to my stomach. 'Harri, let mummy sleep,' he said happily. 'Good girl.'

It touched me when he spoke to her.

'Sit down, sweet chick, and I'll make you decaf. Fancy cheese on toast?'

'Oh yes, please.' I smiled and sank heavily into the chair at the kitchen table.

'What's your plans for today then?'

'I think I'll make us a pasta bake for dinner ... What do you say? I'll work for a little bit before that. Maybe I will be able to finish editing the novel ... I'll bet the author is itching to see the text after the corrections.'

'I am glad that you are doing the editing again. I am sure that freelancing will work out just great after we give birth.'

'I think so too, after WE give birth, ha ha,' I laughed.

'Of course! It's just you and me, baby! WE are in this together,' he said with a smile and placed a cup of coffee and a plate of crispy toast in front of me and kissed my forehead. 'Are you planning to go for a walk?'

'I don't know. Why do you ask?'

'The cot should get delivered between nine and twelve by DPD. It would be good if you could wait for it.'

'Sure, no problem,' I assured cheerfully. I couldn't wait to finish off decorating the room upstairs before her arrival.

Charlie sat down at the table with a cup of coffee with a sigh. I knew him well, and I knew he wanted to tell me something, but he was hesitant to see if it was a good time. Ever since I'd got pregnant, he treated me with extreme care. It usually amused me, but it also irritated me a little.

'Do you want to tell me something?' I asked while eating.

'Well, yeah. Apparently, the prosecutor's office discontinued the proceedings concerning Thomas's death.'

A piece of toast got stuck in my throat, so I started coughing.

Charlie looked at me with concern. For obvious reasons, I didn't tell him what really happened a year ago. All he knew about Harris was that he was my mother's old friend. But the truth was that only I knew that his absence left a void that was more difficult to fill than I expected. In quiet moments, my mind inevitably wandered to the events of that night. Although I now carried new life within me, the darkness still lingered.

'How do you know?' I blurted out after a moment.

'Fiona told me,' he said. 'There was an article about it in *The Evening Telegraph*.'

'The person responsible has not been identified?'

'It looks like it,' he said, and then added regretfully, 'Unfortunately, I have to go to work. Are you going to be okay?'

I rolled my eyes.

'Just go!' I urged him, shaking my head playfully. 'We'll see you in the afternoon.'

'I love you,' he said tenderly, kissing me goodbye.

'And I love you,' I assured. 'See you soon!'

As soon as he'd left, I snatched my laptop. I needed to find the proof that Fiona was right, and Johnson's case was over. It had been a long year since that fateful night at my boss's house. A lot of wonderful things have happened since then, yet I still worried that I would lose it all in an instant.

After scouring the Internet, I finally got what I needed: confirmation of Fiona's words. Relief washed over me like gentle waves on a beach. This meant that John and I could move on with our lives ... There was nothing to stop us from reclaiming our peace.

Tom's case was finally closed. I could finally breathe again, and a huge weight lifted off my chest. But what about Harris? He must be in some far-off corner of the earth, away from any news of this matter. Still, if anyone felt the effects of it, it was him. To ensure his and my safety, he had to drop everything and vanish without a trace.

I decided to go and see Becky in the coming days and talk to her about it. We've grown very close over the past year. She was the first person I told that I was pregnant.

I trusted her implicitly. I knew that she would find a way to reach John with information about the discontinuation of the proceedings. Unfortunately, I had no contact with him.

I slammed my laptop shut and sank deeper into the plush cushion of the couch, finally able to stretch out and take a break from being hunched over. I tenderly caressed my growing bump as I watched my baby dance around under my fingertips. A wave of emotion swept over me at the thought of what was soon to come. I glanced across the room at the framed photograph of my mother, whose eyes seemed to be smiling back at me. A satisfied smirk graced my lips then as I turned to admire the stunning images of myself taken during the pregnancy session. I felt so alive, so incredibly content!

***

Charlie was a totally unexpected blessing. Love had arrived in my life when I least expected it, just at the time after Tom's death. I'd been relocated to the marketing department and found myself working alongside Charlie on a daily basis. We quickly bonded over our shared interests and eventually ended up side-by-side in the same office.

He was the perfect combination of sensitive and funny. He was always there to remind me not to forget about self-care, and he'd rush in to help whenever he could sense I was buckling under stress. Our bond grew stronger with each day, and I couldn't help my rising hopes that he felt the same way too. But I never asked. I knew Charlie was being careful not to pressure me after my mum had just passed away.

Still, weekends without him were awful. Finally, on one Monday morning so desperate for his presence, I flung open the office door and shouted love-struck words from the bottom of my heart.

'I'm a little afraid of how you're going to react to what I'm going to tell you. However, I know that if I don't tell you, my guts will explode with too much emotion.'

He laughed and assured me that he didn't want to collect my insides from the carpet. And then he added:

'If you say it, I'll say it back.'

The rest, as they say, is history.

***

After a few hours of working on the text, I decided to start preparing dinner. Walking to the kitchen and passing the door leading to the porch, I thought I heard a familiar creak. This was the sound my worn-out swing made under the weight of the person sitting on it.

I approached the glass door and looked outside. I blinked, not believing what I was seeing. The next moment I was on the veranda.

'Hi, you cheeky mare,' I heard.

'Jesus Christ!' I burst out happily.

'I told you to call me "John",' he laughed.

'You don't even know how glad I am to see you!' I said with tears in my eyes and walked over to say hello.

'Oh wow, do you need Gaviscon?' he asked, looking at my big belly in surprise.

'What?' I was surprised.

'Gaviscon, supposedly the best for gas and bloating. Don't you know?' He laughed and opened his arms wide to hug me.

'You are an idiot sometimes,' I snorted. Oh, how I've missed our banter!'

'Congratulations, kid!' he exclaimed. 'A girl or a boy?'

'Girl, Harriett.'

'Beautiful name. Sounds like ...'

'Yes, it does,' I butted in, winking at him.

'And do we know the father?' he asked, smiling mischievously.

'Of course, we do! Who do you think I am?!' I laughed again.

'And is he willing to support you both?' he continued the interrogation, very amused. 'Or should I give him a piece of my mind and bury his sorry corpse in the English countryside?'

I waved my hand indulgently and invited my guest for a coffee. He agreed without hesitation. I led him to the kitchen.

'I brought you something,' said John as he took his seat at the table. 'I think you're ready to get to know this story.'

He reached into his backpack and took it out ... Mum's

book!

Tears came to my eyes as I hugged it to my heart. It smelled of promise. It heralded something extraordinary. Eventually, I'll be able to access a part of my mum's past that I didn't have access to before. This day couldn't get any better.

'What have you been doing for the last year, eh?' I asked sometime later when I managed to cool down a bit and make tea for both of us. My hands were still shaking with emotion.

'I'm glad you asked,' he murmured, reaching back into his backpack. This time he pulled out a thick stack of paper tied with a brown shoelace. 'I managed to finish the novel I promised Maya ... Do you know a good editor, by any chance?' he asked with a sneer.

'Maybe I do, maybe I don't, you old fart,' I replied, smiling and holding out my hand toward a new adventure.

Thanks go to:

Graham, Ki, and Lyla for giving me writing space and supporting me during the making of this story. I love you, guys!

Małgorzata, Jonathan, Gary, and Gabriel—for their hard work on the text during the publishing process. For fulfilling all my requests and whims. You guys are awesome!

And to you, my wonderful readers, for your constant support on my writing path. For kind words, reviews, and opinions. You make my writing adventure worth every sleepless night!

I wanted to send you my deepest thanks for purchasing my book! I am so grateful that you took a chance on my writing and supported my work.

Knowing that readers like you enjoy my book means the world to me.

If you wouldn't mind, I would hugely appreciate if you could help spread the word about my book to your friends and family. As an author just starting out, getting the word out about my work is incredibly helpful. The more people hear about the book, the better its chances of success. Please don't feel obligated, but if you're willing to mention it to your inner circle or share it on social media, that would be amazing.

Printed in Great Britain
by Amazon